FOREVER OURS

BOOK ONE OF THE SHATTERED HEARTS SERIES

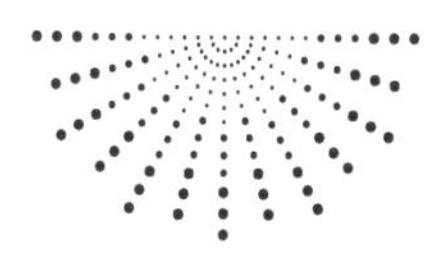

CASSIA LEO

FOREVER OURS

Shattered Hearts #1

by Cassia Leo

cassialeo.com

First Edition

Cover art by Tania Welti.

ISBN-13: 978-1494774301

ISBN-10: 1494774305

ALSO BY CASSIA LEO

CONTEMPORARY ROMANCE

Relentless (Shattered Hearts #2)

Pieces of You (Shattered Hearts *#3)*

Bring Me Home (Shattered Hearts #4)

Abandon (Shattered Hearts #5)

Chasing Abby (Shattered Hearts #6)

Ripped (Shattered Hearts #7)

Black Box (stand-alone novel)

The Way We Fall (The Story of Us #1)

The Way We Break (The Story of Us #2)

The Way We Rise (The Story of Us #3)

To Portland, With Love (The Story of Us #3.5)

To be notified of new books, sign up for Cassia's mailing list at:

eepurl.com/Fgs8T

For all the Chris Knight fans.

This one's for you.

NOTE TO THE READER

Music is an important part of this series. Some chapters in this eBook correspond with songs on the *Forever Ours* playlist. Please feel free to open the playlist on a mobile device or computer and listen as you read.

The playlist is available on YouTube at:
http://bit.ly/foplaylist

The playlist is available on Spotify at:
http://bit.ly/foplaylists

FOREVER INVISIBLE

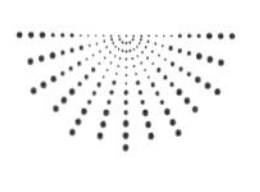

CLAIRE

APRIL 2009

When I was six, my mom told me that fish can breathe under water because they don't have lungs. And she left it at that. What she didn't tell me is that, not only do fish never drown, but they also feel no pain. As I lie down on the filthy concrete behind the grocery store, all I can think is that I want to be a fish.

I wish I could say that I'm homeless through no fault of my own, but that's not true. I'm not homeless. I'm a runaway. There is a slight difference, though the sleeping accommodations are basically the same.

I adjust the pillow under my head as I attempt to get

comfortable. It's not really a pillow. I pulled a cereal box from the dumpster and emptied it out, then I stuffed it with a bunch of discarded plastic grocery bags. I turn my face toward the pillow to smell the box. I never thought I'd actually want a pillow that smells like corn flakes, but it's better than the smell of the dumpster that's standing ten feet away.

It's dark out here. It's 1:30 a.m. If there's anyone left in the grocery store, it's just a couple of employees. I've been coming out here for the past seven nights to sleep. I let myself have a two-hour nap, then I leave. I wander the streets of Raleigh, trying not to feel sorry for myself. I'm a runaway. This is my choice. Then I think of what happened seven days ago — my last day at the Walkers' house.

"Aaron wants to know if you're a virgin."

Lyle grins when he says this. He knows it's going to piss me off. I've been at the Walker residence with Mr. and Mrs. Walker, fourteen-year-old Lyle, and his older sister Stephanie for three days. Three days may actually be a record for me. I think one week is the shortest amount of time it took me to get kicked out of a foster home before this. Lyle's parents must have said something to him about my history, because he seems to think this comment is very amusing.

Aaron is another foster kid who's supposed to be

leaving in a couple of days. The Walkers are getting tired of him hanging out in the bedroom all day with his door locked. I don't blame Aaron. And I highly doubt he's the one who wants to know if I'm a virgin.

"You should tell Aaron that if he wants to know if I'm a virgin, he should sleep with his door unlocked."

Lyle's eyes widen. "Whoa.... You're gonna have sex with him? Just like that?"

"I never said I was going to have sex with him. What I have in mind is much more fun for me than it is for him."

"You're a fucking psycho. No wonder your mom killed herself."

"She didn't kill herself. She OD'd."

"She should *have killed herself."*

When Lyle's mom finally managed to pull me off of him, he had a bloody nose, swollen cheek, and sore crotch. I had a bloody lip, a bump on the head, and a reason to run.

Here I am now, trying to melt into the background of a grocery store. Trying to become invisible. But it's difficult to fade into the scenery when your stomach is growling and your bones ache from sleeping on the hard concrete for seven days. Every movement makes me feel as if my hipbones and ribs are slicing through my delicate skin.

I've lost at least five pounds this week. I can feel it in my clothing. And I didn't really have much weight to spare. One of the consequences of moving from one foster home to the next is that you never really feel comfortable eating. You're always adjusting to someone else's mealtimes and food preferences. I've been underweight for years.

In fact, I'm so underweight right now, I'm convinced this is the only thing that's kept me from being hassled by the cops ever since I left the Walker house. I'm so thin I'm practically invisible. I'm used to being invisible. I actually prefer it. It's the homes where people try to get you to talk about your feelings, or the other kids try to get friendly, that make me want to split.

I'm going to have to find a place to stay soon. When I checked weather.com in the library today, I discovered it's supposed to rain in Raleigh tomorrow. It's the last week of April. Can't we leave the April showers behind us already?

The corner of the cereal box starts digging into my cheek and I lift my head so I can adjust it. That's when I see the police car cruising by. *Shit!*

My heart pounds as I try to force myself to think fast. What am I going to do? I can't run. They'll see me if I try to hide behind the dumpster. Maybe if I just lie still they won't notice me.

The police car stops and the one driving shines his spotlight on me. I cover my eyes with my forearm and he quickly points it a few feet to my left. The car door opens and the tears come instantly as I sit up. They're going to put me in another home with another shitty family that doesn't care if I starve or if their son is a perverted jerk.

"Whatcha doin' back here?" the officer asks as he approaches.

I look up at him for a moment then cover my face to hide the tears. "I'm lost."

FOREVER WAITING

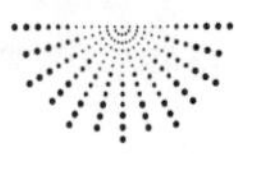

CHRIS

Time stood still the first time I held a guitar in my hands. It was a kind of love that surpassed anything I'd ever felt. I don't know if this means I'm screwed up or just that something broke inside me the day my dad left; and music was the only thing that seemed to fill the empty space. But nothing compares to how I feel when I'm lost in a melody. Even when I'm struggling with lyrics or time signatures, it always feels like I'm exactly where I need to be, doing exactly what I was created to do.

This is why I get really fucking annoyed when Tristan shows up late to practice. I know he doesn't have the best home-life, but I'm eager to get this first set practiced so we can start trying to book gigs. I'm not sure who, if anyone, will take a band of unknown teenagers seriously. All I know is that I won't stop until someone does. Until then, I'll keep waiting for Tristan and hoping for our big break.

"Don't you think this song should be a little more uptempo?" Jake asks as he sits on a stool behind his drum set, reading the notes I gave him for "Hunger," a song I wrote about one of the foster kids my mom took in last year.

I still remember that kid's name: Justin. His mom was addicted to meth and in an abusive relationship. Justin was six years old when they brought him here, and he was skinny as a leaf. His mom kept forgetting to feed him while she was high. These are the kinds of stories I hear all the time ever since my mom started taking in foster children a few years ago. I remember getting so pissed off just thinking about that kid lying in bed, his stomach growling, while his mom was off somewhere getting high or fighting with her boyfriend. I got so angry with my mom for allowing social services to take Justin back to his mom after she got a job and completed her mandatory drug counseling and parenting classes. That's when my mom told me I had to learn to see the situation from the kid's point of view.

All the kids that come through our house love their parents. No matter how shitty their parents treat them. And that taught me a little about love and forgiveness. If a kid can forgive a parent who nearly starves them to death, then I can forgive my father who abandoned me when I was six. Even if he doesn't know I've forgiven him.

"We already have three uptempo songs. This song is about starving. Not exactly an uptempo topic." I plug my electric-acoustic guitar into the amp and sit on the barstool I stole from the breakfast bar in the kitchen. "Where's Rachel?"

"She's at her sister's soccer game."

"I thought she hated her sister."

Jake taps his foot on the bass drum pedal as he continues to leaf through my notes. "Her parents made her go. It's some fucking state championship thing."

"I didn't know she played at that level. No wonder she's hot as fuck." I grab my digital tuner off the coffee table and set it down on my knee so I can tune the guitar. "Is Rachel still gonna play on this one?"

"Yeah, yeah. I already talked to her about it."

The doorbell rings and I'm confused for about four seconds before I remember the call I got from my mom this morning. We're getting another foster kid today. We haven't had any kids for over a month and, truthfully, I've enjoyed the peace. I like being able to practice whenever I want without having to worry if I'm waking up a napping toddler. But they weren't supposed to bring today's kid until four p.m. They're two hours early.

I open the door, prepared to greet the social worker with the usual, *My mom will be here any minute*, but when I open the door Tristan is standing there with Freddy Zimmerman from auto shop class.

"You're late. And why the fuck are you ringing the doorbell?"

Tristan enters ahead of Freddy and they both head straight to the living room with their instruments. Freddy started practicing with us a couple of months ago when I casually mentioned to Rachel that she should play piano on "Hunger." Tristan hates Rachel, so he took it upon himself to invite Freddy over to practice the piano part on his keyboard. I warned Tristan that I didn't want this guy playing that fucking keyboard on any of my songs. His response was to remind me that they're not just my songs.

Tristan sets his bass down on the recliner and his amp on the floor, then he pounds fists with Jake. "I rang the door-bell to make you get your sorry ass up."

"I thought you were a fucking foster kid," I reply, closing the door.

"I thought you guys didn't have any kids right now."

"Nah, we're getting a new one today. A runaway."

"Girl or guy?" Tristan asks, slinging the strap of his bass over his shoulder.

"Girl. I think her name is Claire."

"Maybe they'll send one your age this time," he says, wiggling his eyebrows.

"Nah, an older girl would be better. They know what they're doing," Freddy says, plugging in his keyboard.

I shake my head. No matter how many times I tell them that I'm not allowed to even say anything inappropriate to a foster kid, Tristan still always suggests it.

"You know I can't do that. And you can't talk like that when she gets here or my mom can get cited."

"Whatever. You need to get laid. How long has it been since... what was her name?"

I set the tuner back on the coffee table and settle the guitar in my lap. "Erin. And that was only two months ago."

We run through the song a few times before Tristan decides he's going to try to get the neighbor to buy us some beer. He takes off and I decide to start playing something else. I don't want to give Freddy the impression that Jake and I want him there or that he's part of the band. Rachel's playing the piano on this song no matter how many times Tristan brings this asshole over here.

I grab my electric guitar and plug it in so I can play "Little Wing" by Jimi Hendrix. Jake and Freddy look on as I transition right out of the opening solo into "Stairway to Heaven." About thirty minutes pass before the doorbell rings again, right when I'm in the middle of playing "I Want You" by the Beatles. It's probably Tristan being a dick again.

"Come in!" I shout at the door from where I'm now sitting on the carpet next to the coffee table.

The doorknob jiggles a little then it slowly begins to turn. I knew it was Tristan.

I go back to playing and I'm nearly at the end when I hear the thud of something dropping on the floor behind me. I turn around and a skinny girl with stringy blonde hair and wide blue eyes is staring at us like she just walked in on a fucking murder scene.

FOREVER ASLEEP

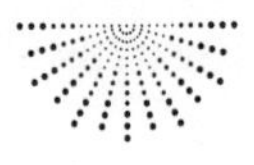

CLAIRE

I'm dead on my feet. I'm so tired I can barely drag myself out of Carol's SUV. I just want to go to sleep and wake up in August when I'm sixteen and I can get a work permit; or in two years and four months when I'll be eighteen—when I age out of the system—and I can say goodbye to foster homes forever.

A woman with short brown hair and round hips comes out of a white van labeled Wickedly Sweet Bakery. She slides the side door open and grabs a pink box off the seat, then she turns on her heel and makes her way toward Carol and me. The smile on her face vanishes the instant she sees me.

"Oh, my goodness," she says with a slight Carolina accent. "You're bone-thin, darling."

I turn away and pretend to adjust my backpack on my shoulder so I don't have to respond to this.

"She hasn't slept all night. I know you just got home from work, but is her room ready?"

"Oh, yes, yes. Everything's all set. Honey, you go on ahead and Chris will show you to your room while I talk to Carol. Here, I'll take that backpack for you."

"I don't need help," I say, backing up as she holds her hand out for me to give her my bag. "I'll just go inside."

I carry my backpack up the front walk of the two-story house in West Raleigh. At least this place is a little nicer than most of the homes I've stayed in. A lot of foster parents are just in it for the money, and the money's not even that great. But I guess to some people, it's better than sitting in an office all day for a little more than minimum wage. One of the foster families I stayed with was pretty nice, until they couldn't understand why I didn't want to hang out and watch Disney movies with their kids all day long. People are inherently greedy. If they take you into their home, it doesn't matter to them that they're getting paid. They want you to get down on your knees and thank them for taking you in. They question why you don't want to eat their shitty meals. Or why you wake up screaming in the middle of the night with the image of your dead mother's body half-hanging off the sofa. There's no privacy. I'm just tired of feeling like an unwanted guest. I want my own home with my own food, my own bed, my own shower.

But I'd give all that up to have my mom back.

I hesitate for a moment before I press the button for the doorbell. Immediately, I hear a male voice shout for me to come in. His mom probably told him to expect me, but he could at least answer the fucking door. I shake my head as I turn the doorknob and slowly push the door open.

My caseworker, Carol, flat out told me that this would be my last placement. If I screw this one up, I'll be sent to a halfway house until I turn sixteen in August. The moment I step into the living room, I know I'll be seeing the inside of that halfway house soon.

Three guys sit around a coffee table, two of them on the sofa and one cross-legged on the floor with a guitar in his lap. The one with the guitar wears a gray beanie and his dark hair falls around his face in jagged wisps. He's humming a tune I recognize as a Beatles song my mom used to play: "I Want You."

The thud of my backpack hitting the floor gets his attention and he looks straight into my eyes. "Are you Claire?" he asks. His voice is smooth with just a hint of a rasp.

I nod and he sets his guitar down on the floor in front of him. My body tenses as he walks toward me. My mom taught me never to trust men or boys. She was so candid with me about the ways she was violated by her uncle from the time she was nine until she was fourteen. I followed my mom's advice for eight years and I haven't been so much as hugged the wrong way. I've kept myself safe, but only by getting myself kicked out of every foster home at the slightest hint that someone might see me as prey. This guy in the beanie doesn't look like a predator, but looks can be deceiving.

He grabs the handle of my backpack and nods toward the stairs. "I'm Chris. I'll take you to your room."

I follow him up the stairs and down a hallway to the last door, which stands open, waiting for me. The house smells like a mixture of lavender and cupcakes. It's kind of comforting, but I don't want to get too comfortable here. Chris sets my backpack down on the floor in a plain bedroom with a teddy bear wallpaper border. I'm accustomed to sleeping in bedrooms decorated like a toddler's playroom, so this is nothing new.

"My mom wouldn't let me take that stupid border down," he says, lifting his chin toward the ceiling as he digs his hands into the pockets of his jeans. He's apologizing to me over a wallpaper border? *Great.* I can already tell this guy is going to get too friendly with me.

As he looks up at the wallpaper, I see a thin nose ring dangling from his septum.

"I don't care about the wallpaper. I just want to go to sleep."

His lip quirks up in confusion. "It's three o'clock."

"I haven't slept. I got kicked out last night and I spent the night at the police station. I refuse to sleep in the presence of strangers." It was no surprise to me when the cops took me back to the Walkers' house and they didn't want anything to do with me.

"Afraid someone will shank you in your sleep?" He smiles, so amused with himself, and I notice another piercing in his tongue. This guy thinks he's so fucking cool.

"I'm not having sex with you," I declare, crossing my arms over my chest—not that there's much to hide.

"What the fuck are you talking about?"

"I see the way you're looking at me."

"Yeah, all right. I guess I'll let you sleep and maybe when you wake up you'll chill the fuck out and realize that just because someone's nice to you it doesn't mean they want to fuck you."

My eyes widen at these words. I want to tell him to get the fuck out, but I'm dumbfounded.

He sees my shock and his face softens. "Or you can come downstairs and hang out and maybe I'll play you a song."

FOREVER PRACTICING

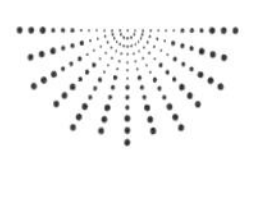

CHRIS

She doesn't saying anything, but I can see that she's interested. She's probably never had anyone offer to play a song for her. Something about her is strange. As I step aside for her to leave the room ahead of me, I can't shake the feeling that I've seen her somewhere. Maybe we went to the same school at some point.

"Do you go to ADHS?" I ask as she descends the stairs.

"I went there for a couple months last year until I got moved to a home in Durham."

Her voice sounds a little scratchy, like she's been screaming at a concert or sporting event all day long. She's probably just thirsty, or hungry judging by the way her T-shirt and jeans hang loosely.

"You want something to drink. We've got orange juice, Capri-Sun, milk, and water. And coffee, if you're into that."

She steps down into the foyer and Tristan is back with a six-pack of Bud Light. "Put that away. My mom's outside."

"Fuck," he whispers, tucking the six-pack behind one of the throw pillows on the blue sofa. "Who's this?"

"Hey, everyone, this is Claire." I look to her and she looks so uncomfortable. She's looking everywhere but at my friends. "We should probably finish up tomorrow. My mom will be here in a minute."

"Are you kicking us out?" Tristan says, the left side of his mouth turning up. He probably thinks I'm telling them to leave so I can try to hook up with Claire.

"Yeah, get the fuck out. We'll pick up where we left off tomorrow. But Rachel will be here, so don't get any ideas."

Tristan rolls his eyes and I lead Claire into the kitchen while they pack up their shit.

"You can grab anything you want. There's nothing off limits." She stands next to the breakfast bar staring at the fruit bowl on the counter. "My mom will probably ask you to make a list of stuff you need from the store; food, shampoo, all that girl stuff."

She looks almost as surprised as she did when I told her I didn't want to get in her panties.

"*Anything* I want?"

"Yeah, I guess. I mean, I don't think you can put ponies on layaway at Walmart, but I'm sure she'd try if you put that on your list." This gets a faint smile out of her. "My mom will be in here soon and she'll probably want to cook something for you."

Something about this makes her hang her head. "I'm not hungry."

"Look, no offense, but you look like you haven't eaten in days."

"No offense?" She looks up at me. "Telling someone they look like they're starving probably doesn't sound that offensive, but it is."

"Sorry. I just.... Well, you don't have to eat, but my mom makes dinner every day whether you want to eat it or not."

"Just a typical American family, huh?"

"Yeah, I don't know what that means." I open up the refrigerator and reach into the box of Capri-Sun to pull out a pouch for her. Shit. It's the last one. "Here." I place the drink on the breakfast bar in front of her. "We can hang out in the living room while my mom cooks. Unless you want to go to bed."

"I thought you were going to play your guitar or something."

I smile even though she looks dead serious. "Yeah, we'll wait until these assholes leave."

Jake is waiting just inside the front door as Tristan and Freddy haul their equipment across the living room. "See you later, man," Jake says with a nod. "I'll give Rachel that sheet music."

"And the notes," I reply and he nods. "See you tomorrow."

"Peace out," Freddy says and I nod at him and Tristan as they all leave.

I grab my guitar off the carpet and nod toward the sofa. "You can sit down. My mom will be in here soon." I feel the need to keep reminding her of this so she doesn't think I'm going to try anything. As much as my friends suggest this to me, I'm sure she's encountered enough creeps in the foster homes she's been in before this one.

She sits on the side of the sofa where Tristan tucked the six-pack of beer behind the pillow. I hope he took it in one of his cases. I don't want to have to sneak that shit into the garbage.

I take a seat on the recliner and lay the guitar in my lap. "What do you want to hear?"

She shrugs. "I don't care."

"Do you mind if I play something I've been trying to practice? It will probably sound like shit."

"By all means, play your shitty song."

I laugh and she smiles; a tight-lipped smile, like she's trying not to. "Now I don't want to play it because it's definitely not a shitty song. I just haven't learned to play it well yet."

"Just play the song."

The way she says this makes my heart race, and suddenly

I'm nervous. I'm never nervous about performing a song unless it's an audition, which I've only been on two of those. *Crap.* I'm going to fuck up this song. I know it.

I draw in a deep breath and position the guitar in my lap. Curling my fingers around the fret board, I decide to play this one without a guitar pick.

As soon as I begin plucking the strings, the nerves subside and I give myself up to the song. I've been practicing "In Your Eyes" by Peter Gabriel since last week. Every time I've played it up to now, I've messed up on the bridge. I'm notorious for messing up the bridge of every new song I play. But this time I don't mess up and I find myself grinning uncontrollably as I sing the last line.

I hold my hand down on the strings to stop the lingering reverberation and I finally look up from the guitar. My mom is standing next to the sofa where Claire is seated and they're both staring at me, unblinking. I wait a moment for one of them to say something and I'm not surprised when it's my mom who speaks first.

"Didn't you just start playing that last week?"

I nod and look back down at my guitar as that nervous feeling returns. I sense an embarrassing comment coming from my mom about how proud she is of me or how talented I am. I don't want to look up and see Claire's reaction to this comment.

"That was beautiful," my mom continues, and I sigh with relief. "What do you two want for dinner?"

I look at Claire and I'm surprised to find she's crying. "Are you okay?"

My mom looks down at her and covers her mouth. "Oh, honey. I'm sorry. I didn't even ask you how you're feeling."

Claire shakes her head as she hides her face. "Sorry. I don't know what's wrong with me."

"You're just tired. That's all. You can have dinner with us or you can go straight to bed. Whatever you want to do. The bedroom's all ready for you." She turns to me with a severe look. "It's ready, isn't it, Chris?"

I nod as I get up from the recliner and set down the guitar. "I got it ready this morning as soon as you called."

My mom kneels down next to the sofa and gently lays her hand on Claire's knee. "Sweetie. You don't have to stay down here if you feel more comfortable upstairs. I can bring your dinner up there later."

Claire pulls her hands away from her face and wipes at the tears that are still streaming. "It's okay. I'll eat down here. Thank you."

"For what?"

Claire looks taken aback by this question, then she shrugs. "For being nice."

FOREVER AWKWARD

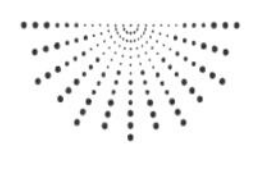

CLAIRE

My first week with Jackie and Chris Knight is the least awkward first week I've ever had in a foster home. Jackie and I spent Sunday, the day after I arrived, running all over town to make sure I have everything I need. Then she took me to Athens Drive High School on Monday to get me registered and I began classes on Tuesday.

Walking into a new school is always nerve wracking, but walking through those front gates with Chris on Tuesday morning made everything less awkward. He has so many friends and most of them are just as nice as he is. They greeted me like I was one of them. Which is why I didn't hesitate when Chris asked if I wanted to sit with them in the cafeteria for lunch.

Rachel and I are the only girls in the group, but she

didn't look too relieved to have another girl join them. But Chris was pretty good at diffusing the awkward questions that are inevitable in my situation. When his friend Tristan asked if I was going back to my parents soon, Chris answered for me. "She's going to be with us for a while."

A couple of days later, when Rachel asked if I had any siblings, Chris's reply made me blush. It was just a simple *no*, but the way he looked so uncomfortable with her question gave me butterflies. I may be totally wrong, but I feel as if his response was meant for me.

And the way they talk about music, especially Chris, is awe-inspiring. I've never heard kids my age talk about the future the way they do. I've heard some of my foster siblings talk about college and getting jobs, but the way they talk about music is not at all like that. It's like a calling for all of them—even Tristan who seems to have fallen into playing the bass sort of by accident.

The only thing I didn't like about hanging out with Chris and his friends this week was how temporary it all felt. Jake and Rachel are graduating in three weeks. And I'm getting a strong feeling that Chris wants to drop out of high school after this school year ends. If I manage not to get myself kicked out of the Knight house by the end of the summer, will his friends still consider me "one of them" if he's gone?

When I come down from my bedroom on Saturday morning, Jackie has gone to work at the bakery, as usual.

She usually leaves for work around four a.m. and returns sometime between four and seven p.m. Chris and I take the bus to school every morning, though he claims he's going to get a motorcycle on his birthday in four weeks so we can get around while his mom is gone. The thought of being that close to him, straddling a motorcycle and wrapping my arms around his waist, makes me nervous. But it seems like no big deal to him.

Chris is sitting at the kitchen table with a bowl of something yellow that may be scrambled eggs and a glass of something white. Mr. Miyagi, his ten-year-old Shiba Inu, is sitting at his feet panting as he waits patiently for Chris to slip him a treat. Chris grimaces as he brings a spoonful of the yellow food to his mouth.

"What are you eating?" I ask, wondering if maybe Jackie left us some breakfast to heat up before she left. She does that often.

He swallows the food and shakes his head at me. "The worst scrambled eggs I've ever had. They taste like ass."

"You know what ass tastes like?" My eyes widen as I realize what I just said and he laughs. "I mean, did you make them?"

"Yeah, I tried to make them the way I saw my mom make them, but I think I might have forgotten a step."

I step closer to the table to peer down into his bowl and I try not to laugh. "I think you forgot the step where you cook the eggs. Those scrambled eggs are practically raw. That's disgusting."

He narrows his eyes at me, looking slightly offended. "Can you make better scrambled eggs than this?" I don't answer right away and he answers for me. "I didn't think so."

I chuckle as I grab his bowl of eggs. "I'll make you some real scrambled eggs. It's one of the few things I know how to make. What are you drinking?"

He grabs his glass off the table and follows me into the kitchen. "It's a banana protein shake. It's not so bad."

I place his bowl in the sink then head for the refrigerator to get the carton of eggs. "A protein shake and eggs? Are you trying to build muscle?"

He's silent for a moment. When I look at him, he looks like he's calculating a response. "Why? Do you think I need to build muscle?"

I laugh as I set the carton of eggs on the counter and reach into the cupboard beneath the counter for a large bowl. "No, I'm just curious. That looks like a body builder's breakfast."

"You know a lot of body builders?"

"No, but I've had some foster siblings who were into that."

He stands next to me as I crack the eggs into the bowl, taking each discarded shell and tossing it into the garbage for me. His arm and hand keeps brushing against mine and I have to keep taking deep breaths every time he turns away to calm my nerves.

"Have you ever…?" He shakes his head as he seems to decide not to finish this question.

"Have I ever *what?*"

"Nothing. Do you need the salt or something?"

I don't press him for an answer. I finish making us some scrambled eggs and we eat in relative silence until he asks me something that catches me totally off-guard.

"Do you miss your mom?" I clench my jaw and stare into my bowl as I try to think of an appropriate response. "I'm sorry. You don't have to answer that. I just…. My dad left when I was six and…. Anyway, it doesn't matter. Just forget I asked."

I nod my head and when I look up from the bowl he's looking straight at me. "Yeah. I miss my mom."

He smiles at this answer, but something about his smile makes me feel like I've shared too much with him. I quickly wipe at the tears that begin to fall, then I bolt up from the table to take my bowl to the sink.

"I have to clean up."

He quickly stands up after me and follows me into the kitchen. "You don't have to do that. I'll clean up. You cooked."

He catches up to me at the sink and squeezes in next to

me so he can do the dishes. As soon as his arm grazes mine, the tears come faster.

"Hey," he says, grabbing my elbows so he can turn me toward him. "My mom always says that the easiest, cheapest gift you can give someone is a hug." He holds out his arms and beckons me. "Come here."

I stare at him for a moment, then I let out a deep sigh and allow him to take me into his arms. My arms feel awkward at my sides, so I slowly raise them and wrap them around his waist. I feel him let out a breath, as if he were waiting for that, then I cry. I cry on his shoulder for so long, I know he must think there's something deeply wrong with me. But he doesn't mention it. In fact, he just encourages me, telling me every so often to let it go and that it's okay to feel this way.

And I believe him.

FOREVER CURIOUS

CHRIS

Normally, Tristan accompanies me to all my tattoo sessions. This time, I decide to take Claire. Tristan would have to ask his grandma to drop him off here first. My tattoo artist, Shayla, lives just half a mile away from our house. It's 1:30 p.m. Today was an early day at school and they let us out at 12:45. Claire and I can walk the mile to her house and be back in time before my mom gets home from work tonight. I hope we'll be back by then.

"Your mom won't be mad about you getting a tattoo?" Claire asks as we set off away from the house toward the main road.

"She won't be mad if she doesn't find out."

The fourth Wednesday of May is warm and sunny with the occasional breeze that blows Claire's blonde ponytail into her eyes every so often. I find myself stealing glances at the spot on her neck where her hairline melts into her nape. It looks so soft. And the way the sun radiates off of every inch of her makes me wish I could touch her glowing skin.

"How many tattoos do you have?"

"I only have four tattoos, so far, but each one is special to me." I push up the sleeve on my left arm to show her the electric guitar that's wrapped in a bar of music from one of my favorite songs, "Little Wing" by Jimi Hendrix. Then I hold out my left forearm for her to see the antique stop-watch tattoo with the hands stopped at 3:15 p.m., the time it was when my father left. "You've already seen this one. Then there's this one on the back of my neck." I show her the Chinese characters on the back of my neck that spell out, *What we think, we become*. "I have one more on my chest."

I don't ask her if she wants to see it, but I watch her face for her reaction. She glances at the cars passing by on Avent Ferry Road, then she looks back at me. I can see she's contemplating whether or not she wants to see it.

"What kind of tattoo is it?"

"It's stupid."

She smiles. "What do you mean? All those other tattoos were really cool. I'm sure it's not stupid."

"No, really. It's probably the stupidest tattoo I've ever seen on anyone. This is the tattoo that got me in trouble. I got it while Tristan and I were super drunk a couple of months ago and my mom flipped when she saw it. Then she made fun of me for weeks."

"Okay, now I have to see it."

I smile and shake my head. "Nope. I'm getting it covered up soon and you'll never know what it was."

"Aw, come on. That's not fair."

"Why?"

She shrugs and turns her gaze back to the sidewalk ahead of us. "I don't know. Tristan got to see it."

My heart races at this reply, which implies she wants to be as worthy as my best friend. "All right. I'll let you see it when we get to Shayla's."

"*Shayla*? Your tattoo artist is a *girl*?"

"Is that a problem?"

She shakes her head, keeping her eyes focused straight ahead. "Nope. Just assumed it was a guy." She clears her throat and digs her hands into the pockets of her skinny jeans. "So why are you getting a tattoo today?"

"It's my birthday today."

She whips her head toward me. "It's your birthday? Why didn't you say anything at lunch?"

"I didn't expect anybody to remember. Tristan and Jake are the only ones who know my birthday, but it's not like I made them set reminders on their calendars or anything. It's just a birthday. It's not a big deal."

She looks disappointed with this response. "So, you're sixteen now?"

"Yep. Sweet sixteen." I wink at her and she blushes as she turns her attention back to the street. "Can I ask you a question?"

She sighs as if she already knows what I'm going to ask. "You can ask whatever you want. I can't guarantee I'll answer."

"Fair enough." I pause for a moment as I work up the courage, then I spit it out quickly. "Have you ever had a boyfriend?"

"One. When I was twelve."

"Twelve?"

"We were only together for, like, four days."

"What was his name?"

"Why do you want to know?" She's still looking straight ahead, but she's wearing a whisper of a smile.

"Because I want to know everything about you."

FOREVER ENVIOUS

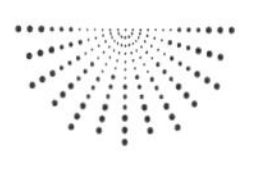

CLAIRE

We arrive at 424 Helms at that moment and I gladly accept the momentary distraction to catch my breath as Chris bounds up the porch steps to ring the doorbell. *Oh, God.* Even the way he rings the doorbell looks cute. How he glances at me over his shoulder, his face beaming with excitement over some new ink. Like a kid on Halloween waiting for someone to answer the door and dump candy into his bucket.

I turn away quickly before he can catch me swooning. Looking out at the two-story houses on Helms Avenue, I'm reminded of a house I lived in last year, just a few streets away from here. I was there for four months during the summer and the end of my eighth grade year. My birthday came and went that year without anyone noticing, even after I'd lived with the Grohl family for a few months. It wasn't as if this was the first time my birthday was forgotten. It was that I had promised myself that I would have the courage to say something this time. And I didn't.

I really hope it doesn't happen again this year. I don't think I could handle another forgotten birthday. Not in the Knight house.

"Claire!"

I turn around at the sound of Chris's voice. My stomach clenches as he nods toward the open door where a beautiful girl who can't be more than twenty years old stands. She raises her eyebrows as she waits for me to join them.

Chris moves aside so I can enter before him. "Claire, this is Shayla. Shayla, this is Claire."

"This your girlfriend?" Shayla asks in a bored voice.

Her pink hair is short and spiky, but her skin and makeup are flawless. Her tank top shows off her smooth tattooed arms. And her skinny black jeans are riding so low, I can see the waistband of her lacy panties.

I take a seat on the sofa as Chris and Shayla make their way a bit further into the room so Chris can sit on a chair. The mint-green vinyl chair sits in the middle of a wood floor in what should be a dining area, and looks like it was stolen out of a dentist's office. The far wall behind the chair is mirrored from floor to ceiling and the wall on the right is lined with shelves holding disinfectant, inks, and various supplies.

Without any warning or prompting, Chris peels off his T-shirt. His chest and ab muscles flex as he sits on the chair. He glances at me as he lies back and smiles when he catches me staring at him. But, mercifully, he doesn't call me out on it.

I watch silently as Shayla grabs stuff off the shelves and begins setting up the machine. But I can feel Chris watching me. Finally, I look at him and he smiles as he beckons me with his finger.

My stomach flips and I take deep breaths as I stand from the sofa and walk to him. Trying not to focus too much on whether or not I have an awkward walk or if my hair looks windblown. Or how much prettier Shayla looks when she walks.

"I told you I'd show you my sorry ass tattoo before I get it covered up," he says when I'm almost next to him.

I stop a few feet away, trying to look anywhere but his chest, but he beckons me closer.

"Come here."

I step forward until I'm right next to the chair. He points at the right side of his chest as Shayla sits down and rolls her chair over the wood floor until she's next to me. When I see the tattoo, I laugh out loud. Uproarious, gut-busting laughter. Right over his left pectoral muscle, spelled out in a drunken scrawl, is his name, Chris.

"You don't have to laugh that hard," he says, though he can't hide his grin.

"I'm sorry." I cover my mouth and try to catch my breath. "Were you afraid you'd forget your name?"

"Ha-ha. Very funny. I was drunk. And I *did* forget my name for a moment. So Tristan said, 'I bet you wouldn't forget it if it was tattooed on you like every other fucking thing you want to remember.'" I shake my head as he looks up at me with the most adorable look of embarrassment. "And I was drunk," he adds again, in case I forgot.

"Maybe you should have just tattooed 'I was drunk' on there," I reply and his eyes light up.

"Shit! Why didn't I think of that?"

I scoot out of the way so Shayla can roll her stool closer to Chris. My heart pounds with roaring jealousy as she wipes the left side of his chest with antiseptic. Finally, I tear my gaze away and head back to the sofa.

When it's over, Chris shows me the tattoo of a monkey sitting down with its eyes closed and legs crossed and wearing a red cape. Chris explains that he has a thing for Japanese culture and the monkey was revered in depictions of Shinto Buddhist mythology.

"Why the red cape?" I ask, as we walk back home.

"Why not?"

I smile and we're silent for quite a while before I clear my throat to speak. "His name was Wade."

"What are you talking about?"

"My boyfriend. The one you asked me about earlier."

"*Wade?*" He looks incredulous. "Are you *serious?*"

"Yes."

"That's a *terrible* name."

"It is not."

"Yes, it is. Claire and Wade? That's just wrong." He smiles and I quickly face forward so he can't see the effect it has on me. "Chris and Claire... Now that's the sound of destiny."

"Wade was very cute." I glance at him sideways to see his reaction and he's looking straight at me, smiling as if he knows I'm trying to make him jealous.

"You want me to help you write a song for Wade?"

"Shut up."

"Wade would never write you a song, but I've already written you three."

I can hardly breathe as my heart pounds crazy fast inside my chest. I glance at him again and his smile has softened.

"If you don't tell my mom about this tattoo, I'll play one of your songs for you."

"I'm not going to tell your mom," I reply quickly.

I want to hear those songs. Now.

He chuckles as we approach the house. "She can be very convincing."

I smile as I think, *Just like you.*

FOREVER BLUE

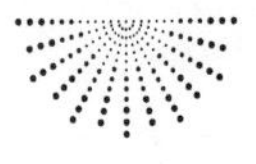

CLAIRE

I wake the morning of June 7th feeling heavy. It's a familiar feeling. It happens once in a while without warning, but it always happens on June 7th. Like a trusty friend who always visits on a special anniversary. My heart is always heaviest on the anniversary of my mother's death.

That's why I always try to do something that makes me happy on June 7th. Wallowing in my room only makes the heaviness worse. I need something light to pick me up.

Last year, I walked to the local movie theater by myself and watched a comedy. Then I stopped and got myself some frozen yogurt on the way back. Mrs. Grohl slipped me a twenty-dollar bill and a look of immense pity when I told her why I wanted to go to the movies.

I wonder if Chris is busy today.

I head downstairs to the kitchen after I've showered and dressed. I've been applying a bit of makeup the past couple of weeks since our trip to Shayla's house. Not that I think Chris prefers Shayla's thick black eyeliner and perfectly pink pout to my natural look. My reason for putting on makeup is even more pathetic than that.

I've convinced myself that by wearing makeup when I'm around Chris, he'll know that I care about what I look like around him. And that, one day, he'll tell me how beautiful I am without makeup. Pathetic. I know.

It's almost three in the afternoon now. I woke up late today and decided to read in bed for a while before I took a shower. *A while* turned into three hours. So this is the first time I've been downstairs all day. I'm starving.

I immediately head for the fridge to make myself a sandwich, when I notice Chris in the backyard, playing with Mr. Miyagi. That poor dog is ten years old and Chris refuses to believe that he doesn't have the same amount of energy as he did when he was a puppy. But watching them through the window, Chris lying on the grass with Mr. Miyagi jumping and barking at him, it makes my stomach swirl with happiness.

Maybe I don't have to go anywhere today.

I grab all the stuff for my sandwich, then I peek my head out the sliding glass door into the back yard. "Do you want a sandwich?"

Chris tackles Mr. Miyagi and proceeds to rub his belly. He looks up at me with a huge smile, tongue practically wagging, then he nods.

I fix us both a sandwich and head outside with our plates. It's a beautiful summer day. So different than it was eight years ago.

I set the plates down on the wrought iron patio table, then I pull out a chair and sit down to eat. Chris heads over to join me and I get a strange feeling in the pit of my belly as I imagine him leaning over to kiss me to thank me for the sandwich. But he doesn't do that. He just sits down and smiles at the sandwich, then he looks up at me.

"Thanks. Did you just wake up?"

I wait for him to take a bite of his sandwich first. "No. I've been reading."

"What are you reading?" he asks through a mouthful of food.

"Just a book. How's the sandwich?"

"Delicious."

I take a bite and realize I forgot the mustard. We eat in silence for a few minutes before I work up the courage to ask him what I wanted to ask.

"Are you going to Tristan's today?"

"Nah, they're coming over here. Why? You want to go to Tristan's?"

I chuckle weakly. He knows I don't get along with Tristan very well.

"I'm kidding," he says, putting his sandwich down. "Do you want to hang out?"

I wait a moment so I don't seem too eager, then I nod. "Yeah. Sure. I mean, today's ... the anniversary of the day my mom died, so I usually do something."

He seems torn between being excited about doing something and pitying me the way Mrs. Grohl did.

"You don't have to feel sorry for me," I continue. "I just thought maybe you'd want to hang out or something. If not, that's totally cool."

"I'd love to hang out. Can I take you somewhere on my bike?"

"No," I reply quickly and he laughs. "Sorry, but that thing scares me."

"All right. We'll stay in." He stares at me across the table. Finally, he smiles. "I know what we're going to do. And we'll do it right here."

Something about the way he says that sounds a little naughty, but I try not to blush. Instead, I take our plates inside and wash the dishes while he gives Mr. Miyagi a bath in the upstairs bathroom. We watch TV for a while as the dog naps on the sofa between us. As requested, Chris doesn't say anything to his mom about today being the anniversary of my mom's death. Just before nine, Jackie goes upstairs to take a bath and go to bed so she can get up at four a.m. for work the next morning.

"Don't stay up too late," she says as she heads up the stairs.

Chris and I don't usually stay up too late. It makes me nervous being alone with him when I'm sleepy. Like I'm going to say something stupid.

"Let's go," Chris says, nodding toward the backyard.

Mr. Miyagi leaps off the sofa at Chris's command and I follow after him. "What's outside?"

He opens the sliding glass door and waits for me to exit before him. "Just wait right here and I'll be right back."

He heads back inside the house, then he returns a few minutes later carrying a patchwork blanket and a couple of pillows. And a guitar. He lays the blanket and pillows down on the grass and motions with his hand for me to sit down.

I take a seat on the edge of the blanket and hug my knees to my chest. He sits next to me and smiles as he pulls the guitar into his lap. He plucks the strings a bit as he tunes the guitar, then he looks up with a soft gleam in his eyes.

"I'm going to sing one of the songs I wrote for you. It's called 'Blue Fields'."

I hug my knees tighter as I lay my cheek on my knee and watch him play. The song is actually pretty upbeat and I wouldn't know it was about me if he hadn't told me. The lyrics are metaphorical. And his voice, that soft rasp, is like the ribbon that ties it all together.

But even though the lyrics aren't literal, I'm pretty sure the song is about loving someone as much as you love the sky.

When the song is over, he looks a little embarrassed, so he quickly lies down. "Come on," he says, patting the blanket behind me. "You have to lie down to look at the stars."

I take a deep breath and lay back until my head lands softly on the pillow. Chris's arm is pressed against mine and I find myself wishing there were more parts of him touching me. Then I find myself wishing that I could do this every June 7th for the rest of my life.

"Thank you," I whisper, just loud enough for him to hear.

His arm moves a little, then he grabs my hand and squeezes. "Any time."

When we wake up on the grass at six a.m. the following morning, all I can think is that we're lucky Mr. Miyagi is lying between to us instead of begging to be let out into the backyard. And Jackie isn't the type to check on us in the morning before she leaves to work. So we're safe.

My arms are wrapped around Chris's right arm like a boa constrictor, the dog snuggled between our legs. Chris smiles at me, then we head inside to have breakfast.

FOREVER HOLDING ON

CLAIRE

AUGUST 9, 2009

There are moments in life that you know will be burned into your memory forever. Chris calls these "movie screen moments" — where everything slows down and you know that something important is about to happen that will change the course of the story. He says that the best songs are written about movie screen moments. I don't know if this is true. All I know is that this is one of those moments.

I can feel it in the air. And I know that when I look back, I'll remember everything about this moment in time; the smells, the tastes, the sounds, and the touch. The touch.

Chris and I are both sitting on the carpet with our backs leaned against the sofa, our fingers woven together as MTV plays in the background. This is something we've done every day for the past eight weeks, ever since the night we fell asleep in the backyard. As soon as Jackie leaves for work in the morning, we both get up and have breakfast together. He usually makes me a bowl of cereal or I make us both some scrambled eggs. Then we hang out in the living room for a few hours until his friends come over. Sometimes, Chris plays his guitar for me. Sometimes, we sit here and pretend to watch MTV, holding hands while Mr. Miyagi lays out across both of our laps, begging to be petted. Well, I don't know if Chris is pretending to watch MTV, but I know I am.

All I can seem to think about when I'm near Chris is whether or not this will last or if he will be just another person I have to lose. But this doesn't stop me from enjoying these hours spent together. I've never been happier in all my life. Not even when my mom was alive.

I'll admit. I was sort of hoping today would be different than all the other mornings Chris and I have hung out. Not that I don't like this small moment of closeness we share every day. But today's August 9th. My sixteenth birthday.

I guess I figured that would make today even more special for us. I was kind of hoping I might get my first kiss.

"Tristan's coming over in half an hour and we're going to the mall. You want to come?"

My heart sinks a little. Chris knows that Tristan and I don't get along very well. He hasn't even wished me a happy birthday and now he's leaving to hang out with Tristan.

I try to let go of his hand and he tightens his grip. "What's wrong?"

I attempt to pull my hand away again and this time he lets go. "I don't want to go to the mall."

"Are you okay?"

I stand up and he immediately stands with me. "I'm just tired. I think I'm gonna go back to bed."

I take a few steps, but he grabs my hand to stop me. When I look over my shoulder at him, he's wearing a crooked smile. "Can you take Mr. Miyagi upstairs with you?"

My shoulders slump as I turn toward Mr. Miyagi where he's lounging on the sofa.

Chris chuckles. "I'm only kidding. I'm not going anywhere with Tristan today. I'm taking you for a ride."

"What?"

"On my bike."

"I'm not going on that thing."

Chris got his motorcycle license the week after he turned sixteen less than three months ago. He's been trying to get me to ride with him on his crappy racing bike ever since the first time I let him hold my hand.

"Come on," he pleads. "I have something I want to show you, but I want to do it alone. I don't want to ask Tristan to take us. Please?"

I stare into his eyes for a moment and he tilts his head. His brown hair always looks calculatedly messy, the way it's just long enough to cover his ears yet still sticks out in all the right places. His skin is so smooth; I often find myself wishing I could press my lips to his cheek just to feel the softness of his skin. And don't even get me started on the metal stud in his tongue. The way he plays with it when he's tuning his guitar makes the butterflies in my stomach cry tears of joy. I don't know what Chris sees in me other than the way my hand seems to fit so perfectly in his.

He pulls me a little closer and lifts my hand to his mouth. My heart races as he lays a soft kiss on my knuckles. "Claire, it's your birthday. And I know you probably haven't had a whole lot of birthdays you want to remember for the rest of your life, but I want this birthday to be the one you never forget. Let me take you for a ride."

I stare at his lips as he says these words and that's when it happens. This is that moment; the moment where everything slows down and nothing is ever the same.

FOREVER FLOATING

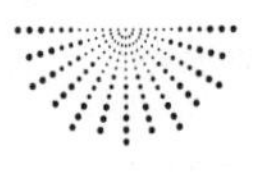

CLAIRE

Chris pulls the motorcycle out of the garage and onto the street in front of the driveway because I'm afraid we'll fall if he goes down the driveway with both of us on the bike. It's a regular old racing bike that he picked up from a neighbor's house on his birthday; the day I went with him to Shayla's house.

The body is lime-green with a black racing stripe that's peeling off. He claims he's already saving up for a new bike. And if he can just score a few well-paying gigs this year, he'll get it for his next birthday.

"Come on."

He nods toward the back of the bike as he squeezes the handlebar and revs the engine. The exhaust pipe coughs out a small cloud of gray smoke that smells like gasoline. He pats the seat behind him and smiles.

I double-check the strap on the helmet Chris bought for me a couple of weeks ago, then I grab his waist and swing my leg over the back of the bike. My stomach vaults when my body is pressed against his back.

"Hold on tight!" he shouts so he can be heard over the sound of the engine and through both of our helmets.

I lean closer to him and wrap my arms tightly around his waist. He reaches back and slides his hand down the side of my thigh until his hand is behind my knee. Then he pulls my leg up to prop my foot on the spoke. He does the same with my other leg and I can hardly breathe from the embarrassment as something pulses between my legs. It's the engine. It has to be rumble of the engine.

He grabs both my hands and pulls them tighter around him, then he gives me a thumbs-up. Now we're all set. *Great.*

I close my eyes and lean the side of my helmet against the back of his right shoulder. I let out a soft scream when he takes off, but I'm quiet the rest of the way. He takes it easy on me the whole way there; going extra slow on the turns and easy on the acceleration. But I'm still ecstatic when he arrives at Moore Square in downtown Raleigh.

My thighs are still humming from the vibration of the motorcycle engine as I stand next to the bike, waiting for Chris to remove his helmet. He hangs his helmet from a hook inside a compartment hidden beneath the seat cushion.

Then he turns to me and smiles as he reaches for the strap on my helmet. The tips of his fingers are a bit calloused, probably from playing the guitar without a pick. He hates using guitar picks when he's practicing.

Goosebumps sprout over my arms and I try not to look at his face as he finally gets my helmet strap unhooked. He gently lifts the helmet off my head and I can feel him staring at me. I bite my lip and try to regulate my breathing. This is it. He's going to kiss me.

I muster the courage to look up into his eyes and he lets out a soft chuckle. "You did good. I think I only heard you scream once," he says, and I let out the breath I was holding as he turns around and hangs my helmet on the same hook where he hung his.

He locks up the seat compartment, then he grabs my hand and nods toward the park area where dozens of white tents are set up for some type of blues music festival. Closer to Blount Street, there are some animal petting zoos set up with billy goats and lambs. The grassy smell of hay hangs thick in the humid summer air as we pass the animal pens.

"You want to ride a pony for your birthday?" he asks.

"I think I stopped qualifying for pony rides when I stopped dotting my I's with hearts."

He laughs and lifts my hand to his mouth to plant a kiss on the backs of my knuckles. "I — That's why I like you."

Suddenly, he looks nervous. As if he almost blurted out something he thought he'd regret.

I squeeze his hand twice before he looks at me. "I like you, too."

He chuckles as he shakes his head. He knows I know what words almost slipped off his tongue. That perfect pierced tongue. And now he knows that I feel the same way.

Oh, God. Please let him kiss me today.

We get to the booths and that's when the fun begins. Chris chats up the vendors at each booth and we learn all about the various types of blues music, from bluegrass and acid blues to R&B and Canadian blues. I never realized how many different genres of blues music there were. The vendors play their music, some of them have musicians in their tents playing. Chris buys me the CDs he thinks I like, or that I *should* like. He's a little pushy when it comes to introducing me to new music. Then we sit on the grass and watch a few bands play on the big stage.

Around six p.m., when Jackie normally gets home from work, Chris's phone rings and he pulls it out of his back pocket. But it doesn't look like his usual phone. It's a brand new smartphone.

He answers the call, then he passes the phone to me. "It's for you."

I'm a little hesitant as I take the phone. "Hello?"

"Happy birthday, sweetie!"

It's Jackie. Something about hearing her voice today gets me all emotional.

"Thank you."

"How do you like your new phone? I hope it's a nice one. Chris wouldn't let me pay for it."

I stare at Chris, then I hold the phone a few inches from my face to get another look at it. "This is mine?"

"Of course! He didn't tell you. Oh, Chris. Always trying to be so sneaky."

I smile at Chris and blink a few times so I don't cry. I've never had a cell phone. And I haven't gotten a birthday present in a few years.

"Thank you," I whisper again because I don't know what else to say.

"You're welcome, sweetie. I'll see you two tonight. Don't be home too late. I have a beautiful cake for you."

I press the red icon to end the call, then I hold the phone in my lap. "I thought you were saving for another bike."

"I'll still get my bike. I've just gotta do a few more gigs. No problem."

His smile is so soft and his brown eyes are so hopeful. I can see that all he wants to know is that this gift made me happy.

"Thank you.... This has been the best birthday... I've ever had."

He reaches up and brushes away the tear that's about to fall from my eye. "You deserve the best."

I smile and take a deep breath, then I hold out the phone to him. "Can you autograph it for me? So it will still be worth something when you're rich and famous."

He smiles as he reaches up and softly places his index finger on my lips. "I'd rather put my signature here."

My heart pounds as he leans toward me. This is it.

His lips land softly over mine and I breathe in the cinnamon scent of the churros we ate earlier. His lips linger there for a moment and I have to remind myself to breathe. Then he kisses me again, parting his lips just a little bit this time. With each kiss, he opens his mouth just a little wider. Until, finally, he slips his tongue into my mouth.

The first thing I taste is sugar, then cinnamon, then the soft metallic flavor of the metal stud in his tongue. That's when I know this is real.

His tongue brushes against mine and I try to mimic everything he does. And I think I'm doing pretty well when he lets out a soft moan. This spurs me on and I reach up to hold the back of his neck.

We kiss like this, just sitting on the grass under the oak trees, for a while. But it's not long enough. When he finally pulls away and lays a soft kiss on my nose, I think my lips are a bit numb.

"Happy birthday, Claire." He plants another kiss on the corner of my mouth. "I love you."

My entire body feels so light and warm, like a hot-air balloon ready to take flight.

I wrap my arms around his neck and lay my head on his shoulder. "I love you, too."

FOREVER ADDICTED

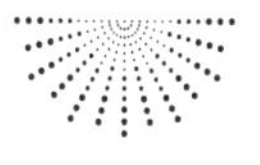

CHRIS

I tumble out of bed and drag myself out of my bedroom and into the hallway. When I push open the bathroom door, my eyes widen at what I've stumbled upon. Claire is standing next to the toilet, holding her new cell phone over the toilet bowl. Her lips are pressed together in a hard line across her delicate face.

"What the fuck?" is the first thing that slips out of my mouth.

"I don't want this thing anymore."

"Please don't drop it in the toilet."

"What is the point of having a cell phone if you never answer it?"

Oh, shit. She's had this phone two months and it's turned her into a crazy person. I don't dare say this out loud, but I'm beginning to wish I'd gotten her something else for her birthday.

If I don't call her back within a few minutes, she accuses me of playing games. If she doesn't call me back right away, it's because she was busy. I don't think she even realizes how insane this sounds.

"What do you want me to do? Just tell me what you want and I'll do it." I inch closer to her and she smiles when she realizes she has my attention. "You want me to promise I'll never wait more than five minutes to call you back? Would that make you happy?"

She loses the smile and purses her lips. "This phone has turned me into an addict. I look at it every two minutes to check for missed calls and texts from you. It's sick!"

I reach for her wrist and slowly move my hand down until the phone is in my hand. I place it gently on the bathroom counter, then I look her in the eyes.

"Babe, you're not addicted to your phone. You're addicted to me."

"Shut up!" she smacks my chest and I try not to laugh too loud.

I wrap my arms around her waist and pull her against me. She's breathing hard as my lips hover over hers. "Don't you have to get ready for school?"

"It's a late day. I don't have to be at school for two and a half hours."

I smile. It actually makes me happy that I can't remember what day is a late day anymore since I quit school. The only regret I have about quitting school is that Claire is alone now. With Jake and Rachel graduated, and Tristan hanging out with his new girlfriend, Ashley, Claire says she spends most of her time outside of class reading.

"Good, 'cause I have plans for you.... I gonna text you for two hours straight."

"You're such a jerk!"

She tries to push me away and I lean in to kiss her. At first she closes her mouth, but she laughs when I plant a loud kiss on her cheek. And I seize the opportunity to kiss her hard.

Seconds later, we're lying on my bed, the sheets bunched up beneath her and my hand easing down her waist to her hip. She grabs my hand to stop me and I smile as I move my hand up. I trail my lips over her smooth jaw and plant a soft kiss on her neck. I hear a sniffing noise and I quickly pull my head back, afraid she's crying.

"Oh, my God. You smell so good," she says, leaning forward so she can sniff my shoulder.

"Really?"

She grabs fistfuls of my T-shirt and brings them to her nose as she inhales. "Yes! Is that some kind of cologne or something?"

"No, it's laundry soap and you use the same one."

"No, it has to be something else."

I reach up and lightly drag my fingertip across her jawline. "Yeah, it's laundry soap and my pheromones, which you obviously can't get enough of. Addict."

"Shut up."

"What? There's nothing wrong with that. I can't get enough of your scent either." I bury my face in the crook of her neck and she lets out a soft gasp when I lick her skin. "You smell sweet and salty at the same time, like raspberries with a hint of the beach. It's fucking intoxicating."

"Really?" she breathes. "That's what I smell like to you?"

I nuzzle my nose against the sensitive spot behind her ear and she giggles softly. "See what you do to me? I can't get enough of you."

I kiss her neck and her skin is so soft, I want to devour her. But I respect her boundaries. So minutes later, we're on my bike on the way to drop her off at school. As usual, she plants a kiss on the front of my helmet, leaving a kiss mark on the glass. Then she bats my hand away when I try to grab her ass as she walks away.

Something about this feels too perfect. I keep waiting for my mom to tell me that Claire's being moved to another foster home. Or that my mom will find out about us and Claire's caseworker will have her removed from our home.

Something bad is coming. It could be next week or next

year. All I know is that this can't continue the way it has. It's too perfect. Nothing in my life has ever been this good or easy.

FOREVER THANKFUL

CLAIRE

DECEMBER 25, 2009

Christmas at the Knight house is quiet and warm; just the way I remember it being with my mom. My mom used to put on the TV to whatever channel was playing the black and white movie marathon. Then we'd decorate the little tabletop tree she set up on the kitchen table with the sound of *It's A Wonderful Life* playing in the background. The only gifts I ever remember getting from my mother on Christmas were a book about the Milky Way and a puzzle of the solar system. I wish I still had that book.

After a huge feast of roast chicken, macaroni and cheese, green beans, and mashed potatoes, I feel as if I might burst.

But I can't let Jackie do the dishes after cooking such a huge spread.

"I can do that," I say, scooting in next to her at the kitchen sink.

Chris sandwiches her on the other side and we gently scoot her back. "Go sit down. We'll do this."

Chris washes while I dry the dishes and put them away. Occasionally, his hand will linger on mine when he passes me a plate or a cup and I have to shoot him a severe look to get him to let go. Jackie doesn't know anything about Chris and me, and we have to keep it that way. I don't know what I'd do if she found out about us and I were placed in another home.

When we're done with the dishes, Chris and I join Jackie in the living room to open presents. Chris gets an expensive motorcycle jacket and a gift card to his favorite music store from Jackie. Chris and I give Jackie a silver bracelet with three emeralds, which makes her cry for some reason. And Jackie gives me a gift card to my favorite book store and a new winter coat.

When it comes time for Chris and I to exchange gifts, my stomach is in knots. I know Chris wouldn't give me anything too expensive or personal. He doesn't want his mom to know about us anymore than I do. But I'm nervous about what he'll think of my gift to him.

"You go first," he says, and I shrug like it's no big deal.

I tear open the wrapping paper on the small box and my heart races. Lifting the lid on the white box, I find another smaller box inside. I open that box and find a small envelope. When I open the envelope, I find a picture of me and my mom.

My mother's sitting on the same sofa where she died. I'm sitting in her lap, my head nestled in the crook of her neck as she kisses my forehead. The picture is too fuzzy to see the track-marks on her arms. We look like a normal mother and daughter.

"How did you get this?" I whisper through the painful lump in my throat.

"I asked my mom to talk to your caseworker and she contacted the lady you used to live next door to when you lived with your mom. This was the only picture she had. Are you upset?"

I shake my head. "Thank you."

"It's a beautiful picture of you two," Jackie adds with a gentle smile that actually makes me feel worse.

Chris begins tearing the wrapping paper away from his gift and I'm grateful for the distraction. When he lifts the lid on the box, he lets out a soft chuckle. He lifts the T-shirt out of the box and holds it up for us to see.

I had to skip lunch at school for a couple of weeks to save up enough money for the shirt, but it was totally worth it. The black T-shirt has a white silhouette of a guy playing the guitar on the front, and the letters CK on the bottom right. The back of the shirt reads, "Music is my religion." A quote from his idol, Jimi Hendrix.

"You made this?"

"Some guy in my English class designed the image on the front," I reply.

"Some guy in your English class?"

I swallow hard when I realize he's jealous, but this is not the right place for him to be jealous.

"Just some guy.... Anyway, I took the design to that T-shirt shop in the mall and they put it on there. Do you like it?"

He looks conflicted, like he wants to address the issue about the guy in English class who designed a shirt for me, but he knows he can't do it with Jackie here. Something about this makes me want to laugh.

"Yeah, I like it."

"Oh, please, Chris," Jackie remarks. "Show a little more gratitude. I think it's a very thoughtful gift."

"It is," he adds, looking me in the eye. "I love it."

He puts emphasis on the word *love* and it makes my stomach flip.

Chris and I stay downstairs to watch a movie while Jackie heads to bed early after a long day of cooking. We always wait at least an hour after she goes up before we let down our guards. When that hour is up, I look at Chris and he's already staring at me from the other end of the sofa.

"So who's this guy in your English class?"

I press my lips together to keep from smiling, but it's too hard.

"You think it's funny?"

"Oh, come on. It's just some guy who sits next to me in English. I noticed him drawing some comics and asked if he could draw something for me."

"What did you offer him in exchange for the drawing?"

"What do you *think* I offered him?"

He's silent as he waits for me to answer the question.

"I offered him five bucks."

"That's it?"

"Yes, that's it. Can we change the subject now?"

He pats the cushion next to him. "Come here." I let out a huge sigh, then I scoot over until I'm next to him. "It drives me crazy knowing you have this whole other life at school."

"You have a whole other life at home. You didn't even pick me up from school all last week because you were doing God knows what with Jake and Rachel."

"Doing God knows what?" he replies incredulously. "We were looking for a cheap sound studio to record a demo. We need some digital files if we're going to book gigs."

"Whatever. The point is that I'm the one who should be jealous. I heard Tristan talking about taking you with him to the ice rink where he met that new girl a couple of weeks ago. I'm not stupid. I know what that means."

"You think I want to hang out with Tristan at a fucking ice rink?"

"I don't know. He's always asking you to go places with him and he always looks annoyed when you bring me. That's why I haven't been going anywhere with you guys lately."

"Fuck Tristan. Don't let his shitty attitude keep you from hanging out. If I ask you to come, it's because I want you with me. And I don't give a shit what Tristan wants."

"But he's your best friend."

"*You're* my best friend."

He doesn't blink after he says this. He just waits for my reaction.

I let out a huge sigh of relief, then I climb into his lap and rest my head on his shoulder.

FOREVER DREAMING

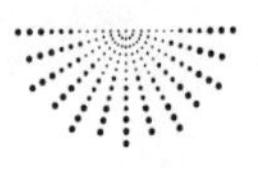

CHRIS

MARCH, 2010

Dreams do come true.

I get the call from John Garrety at one in the afternoon. By two-thirty, I've packed the blue suitcase my mom keeps in the garage and stopped by my mom's bakery to give her the good news.

"Eighteen days!" she cries, slamming down a block of cold butter onto the steel workstation.

The warm, sugary smell of the bakery always reminds me of when I was seven and my mom first bought this place. She used to bring me here after school until I was ten and I insisted I could stay home alone for a few hours after school. I'd sit at a steel table in the corner of the kitchen and do my homework while watching my mom shape bread loaves and pipe frosting onto cupcakes.

My mom's always been a workaholic and a bit of a perfectionist. Which is probably where I get my work ethic. I may have dropped out of school, but that's only because I have bigger things planned for my life than sitting in a classroom and listening to someone drone on about coefficients and revolutionary wars.

My work ethic is what got me, Tristan, and Jake our first mini-tour as the Blue Knights. John Garrety is a promoter for some local blues clubs and a couple of local indie bands. He liked our demo so much, and the fact that we're so young, that he booked us a few shows in Florida and Tennessee. Even without a manager.

I grab the block of butter out of my mom's hand before she can hit me with it. "It's just two weeks and a few days. I'll be back before you know it." She narrows her eyes at me. "And I'll be with Jake and Rachel. You know they won't let me get into trouble."

She shakes her head as if she can't believe what I'm suggesting. "Eighteen days is a long time. What about Claire?"

"What do you mean? She always takes the bus to and from school when I can't take her."

She raises her eyebrows. She wasn't referring to how Claire was going to get to and from school.

"She'll be fine," I assure her.

Her shoulders slump. "Oh, fine. But you'd better call us every morning and night."

"I will." I give her a big hug and some of the powdered sugar on her apron sticks to my T-shirt. "I gotta go. I have to pick up Claire. See you later."

By the time I get Claire home, my stomach is wound so tight I can hardly breathe. I don't know how I'm going to tell her that I'm leaving for eighteen days.

She lays all her books and notes out on the kitchen table to start her homework. I grab a bottle of water out of the fridge for her and place it on the table next to her math book.

"Thanks." She guzzles almost half the bottle in one sip. "What did you do today?"

"I ran around town a little. Actually, I have something I want to show you. Upstairs."

She scrunches her eyebrows together. "Why don't you just bring it down here?"

"I can't. Can you just come up with me for a sec?"

She shrugs and stands from the table. Then she follows me up the stairs to my bedroom. When I open the door, she sees the blue suitcase lying on my bed.

She looks confused and her eyes immediately get watery. "Is that for me?"

"No! Shit! I didn't think this through. No, it's not for you. It's for me."

She clutches her chest and lets out a sigh of relief. "Jesus. You scared the shit out of me. Wait. What do you mean, it's for you? Where are you going?"

I turn to her and grab both her hands. "I'm going to Florida and Tennessee to do a few shows."

Her eyes widen. "Are you serious? Did someone pick up the demo? That's amazing!"

"No, no. Don't get excited yet. It hasn't been picked up, but it did score us a few paid gigs. That promoter I was telling you about a couple of weeks ago set it up."

"So you're just going to play some shows, then you're coming back, right?"

I nod vigorously. "Yes, I'll be back in eighteen days."

"Eighteen days!"

I take her face in my hands and she glares at me. "Claire, it will be over before you know it. You'll probably be glad to have some time away from me." I kiss the corner of her mouth and she shakes her head.

"Why? Are you going to be glad to have some time away from me?"

I keep one hand clasped around the back of her neck as

my other hand drops to her waist, then I lay a soft kiss on her lips. "I'm gonna miss the fuck out of you."

Her lips part as I slide my tongue into her mouth. I tease her a little, sucking on her tongue and her top lip until she lets out a soft, involuntary whimper. I move my hand up the side of her waist and over her ribs until it's brushing up against the bottom of her breast.

"Chris," she whispers into my mouth. "I ... We can't do this."

"Do what?"

I kiss her jaw and the quickened sound of her breathing is getting me excited. I walk slowly backward, pulling her along with me. Then I ease her down onto the bed.

She's trembling.

I tilt my head back so I can look at her face. "Are you okay?" She's staring at my shirt, so I tilt her chin up. "Talk to me."

"I'm gonna miss you."

I brush my thumb over her cheekbone and she smiles. "I'd rather you miss me than forget me."

"Forget you? In eighteen days?" she replies with a chuckle.

I swallow hard and gaze into her eyes for a moment, then I lean in to kiss her. She sucks in a sharp breath as if she's surprised and I slide my hand under her shirt to touch her skin.

"Chris?"

"I want you.... I want to leave you something to think about while I'm gone."

She repeats my name as a soft plea, but her arms tighten around my neck as I kiss her ear.

"I want to invade the space all around you until everywhere you look all you see is me." I trace my tongue along the delicate curves of her ear and she sighs. "I want to occupy the space inside you until you don't know the difference between my heartbeat and yours. I want to be your everything."

I slide my leg between hers and she grabs the sides of my face to push my head back.

"How do you do that?" she asks, her hungry gaze focused on my lips.

"What?"

"How do you always know the right thing to say?"

"I've been practicing that for days."

"You're such a jerk!" She pushes me away and sits up on the bed.

I laugh as I sit up next to her. "I was only practicing because I wanted to get it right. I meant every word." She shakes her head as I lean in to whisper in her ear. "You're my everything. I want to be your everything, too."

She turns to me and her expression is stony. "What

about all the girls that are going to want to be your everything once they see you on that stage?"

I look into her blue eyes and I can't help but smile. "There's no room in my heart for anyone else but you… my Claire-bear."

She rolls her eyes. "There's no room in your heart, but is there any room left in your pants?"

"Not right now." She glares at me and I laugh as she tries not to look at my crotch. "Sorry, but you asked."

She shakes her head and stands from the bed. I stand up after her and she stares at the blue suitcase where it lies on the foot of the bed.

"I'm happy for you," she says, though she doesn't look happy at all.

"For us," I say, grabbing her hand. "Be happy for us. This is just the first step."

"The first step away from me."

"We'll always be together. Even when we're apart. You know it's true."

This elicits a faint smile. "Don't forget me."

"Forget you? In eighteen days?" Her smile widens, so I take her into my arms and kiss her forehead. "It would take at least nineteen days for me to forget you."

FOREVER ALONE

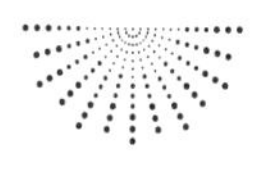

CLAIRE

The worst part of the last eighteen days has been spending my entire Spring vacation alone. Jackie took a day off from the bakery during my week off. She made appointments for us to get manicures and pedicures, but I only went so she wouldn't feel bad. I don't want a mani-pedi. I want Chris.

I feel so stupid admitting that, but it's true. I miss him so much. Even now, as I sit in my English class, he's all I can think of. He's supposed to be back tonight around eleven p.m. or later. I don't care how late he gets home, I'm staying up.

Mrs. Ainsley writes the page numbers of the homework on the whiteboard and I quickly jot it down in the upper right-hand corner of my notebook. Then I slam the notebook shut so I can start packing my backpack. But the moment I twist in my chair to reach for my bag, someone taps my shoulder.

I look up and the sight of Chris's face takes my breath away. "Oh, my God."

"Hey," he says softly, and the sound of his voice, not heard through the static of a cell phone, makes me tear up.

I shoot out of my chair and throw my arms around his neck. "I missed you so much," I say, my voice muffled by the hood of his sweater as I bury my face in the crook of his neck.

He lifts me off the floor and hugs me so tight I can't breathe. "I missed you so much more than that. Next time, you're coming with me."

"Get a room!" someone shouts from behind me and I don't care.

I don't care what anyone thinks or says. All I care is that I have Chris back. His smell, his touch, his voice, his arms. He's back.

He walks me to my locker to get the rest of my books, greeting a few people who've missed him since he dropped out. Then we hop on his bike and I hold on tight as we ride home.

Home.

It's not home without Chris.

As soon as we get to the house, we fall onto the sofa, a

tangle of arms and legs. Kissing, hugging, touching, breathing each other in.

"I've missed your lips," he murmurs.

And for the first time, I find myself wrapping my legs around his hips. He grinds his pelvis into mine and I moan when I feel the hot friction between my legs. Holding his face, I kiss him deeply. Hoping that he can feel just how much I missed him.

Then *I* feel it. Just how much he's missed me.

His erection grows solid beneath his jeans and my heart races. "Chris?"

"I want you so bad." He reaches for the button on my jeans and I grab his hand to stop him.

"Wait."

"Why?"

He looks down at me, confused by my words. I shake my head and he lets out a soft sigh as he sits up. He knows I want to wait until I'm eighteen. It's an irrational self-imposed rule, but I promised myself I wouldn't have sex until I'm eighteen. Even if we're careful, I don't want to end up like my mom, saddled with a kid when I'm just seventeen. Chris knows about my rule. And as I sit up, he winks at me. A small gesture to show he respects it.

"I can wait to have sex with you. But can we do something else? You can leave all your clothes on."

I glare at him because this sounds dubious. "Do what?"

He leans over and whispers it in my ear, though there's no one else around to hear him.

"You want to lick my tongue?" I say out loud. "Isn't that the same as kissing?"

"I guess we'll find out."

I roll my eyes. "Fine. Just get it over with."

"Don't move. Close your eyes and stick your tongue out."

A smile curls the corners of my lips as I let my jaw drop open just enough to stick out my tongue.

"Remember: You can't move, even if you get the urge to touch me. You have to stay still."

I roll my eyes. "Oh, just do it already."

"Okay, stick your tongue out," he whispers so softly it sends a shiver over my skin.

His voice is closer. I can't see anything, but I can feel his breath on the tip of my nose. I stick my tongue out again, a little farther this time, my heart racing as I anticipate the moment of contact. Then I feel it. The tip of his tongue is wet and firm on the tip of mine. A flash of pleasure pulses between my legs as he slowly traces his tongue over mine from the tip to the center. As if his tongue is touching places I've never been touched.

I push him away as I attempt to catch my breath.

"How did that feel?" he asks eagerly.

"Where did you learn that? Were you with someone else while you were gone?"

"What? No! Of course not. I saw it in a movie."

"You went to the movies?"

"It was a movie we saw in the hotel."

"What kind of *movies* were you guys watching?"

"It was just some teen movie from the 80s. I can't remember the name."

The pulsing between my legs slowly dies down, but I can't help but wonder what it would feel like to have him touch me there right now. Or lick me. *Oh, God.*

"I have to go...."

"Where?" he says, standing up after me.

"To the bathroom."

He smiles then licks his lips. "I've missed the taste of your mouth. Hurry up. I want to taste you again."

FOREVER JEALOUS

CHRIS

APRIL, 2011

When I pull my motorcycle next to the curb in front of my old high school, the last thing I expect to see is Claire rolling around on the grass with another guy. I feel as if my insides might explode with rage as I watch them untangle themselves from each other and scramble to their feet. He brushes some grass off her back and she laughs and they both reach for something on the grass at the same time. A piece of paper.

Claire takes the paper from his hand and gazes at it for a moment with a huge grin on her face. Then she appears to thank him and he nods bashfully. She turns around and her eyes widen when she spots me.

She snatches her backpack off the grass and jogs toward me. My heart is pounding as a million thoughts race through my mind. But the most prominent thought is how naive I was. I never thought Claire was the type to even flirt with other guys. And here she is rolling around on the fucking grass.

"What the fuck?" The words come out of my mouth before I can stop them.

"What's wrong?" she asks innocently as she stuffs the piece of paper into her backpack.

She slides her arms through the straps then waits for me to answer her question, or at least get off the bike so we can unlock her helmet.

"What the fuck was that?"

I nod toward the grassy area where she came from.

She glances over her shoulder then turns back to me. "That was just Jason. He gave me a stupid drawing of Sailor Moon 'cause he saw the sticker on my notebook. Can you get off the bike so I can get the helmet?"

"I'm not talking about the drawing. What the fuck were you two doing on the grass?"

"Oh," she laughs. "He was chasing after me to give me the drawing and when he called my name I stopped suddenly. He ran into me and we fell on the grass." She narrows her eyes at me. "Are you mad because we fell on the grass?"

"Does he know you have a boyfriend? Why the fuck he is drawing pictures for you?"

"Are you seriously doing this right now?"

"Answer the fucking question. Does he know you have a boyfriend?"

She glares at me, her nostrils flaring. "You're not allowed to talk to me like that."

She turns on her heel and starts walking toward the bus loading zone.

"Claire, come here." I hop off the bike and quickly catch up to her. "It was a simple question. Why can't you answer it?"

"Leave me alone."

"Come on, Claire. You're not taking the bus over this. Just get on the bike."

I reach for her hand and she smacks my hand away. "Don't touch me."

She climbs the steps onto the bus and I watch as she marches toward the back and plops down on a seat. All the while refusing to look out the window at me.

Fine.

She can get pissy if she wants. It was just a simple fucking question.

I speed home on my bike, then I sit idling in the

driveway for a moment, contemplating whether I should go to the bus stop around the corner to pick her up. Then the image of her and Jason on the grass flashes in my mind. Her laughter. Her smile. The things I thought were only mine.

I rev the engine loudly to drown out the harsh pounding of my heartbeat in my ears.

I pull the bike away from the house, but I don't head to the bus stop. I go to Tristan's instead.

FOREVER FORGIVEN

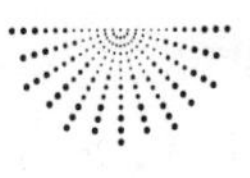

CLAIRE

By the time I step inside the house, I'm sweating profusely from the insane humidity. I close the door then stand completely still for a moment, listening for the sound of a TV or guitar or some type of music. Nothing. The house is cool and silent. Chris is gone.

My stomach aches as I think of the way he spoke to me and where he could possibly be. Probably somewhere with Tristan. He wouldn't cheat on me, would he?

I drop my backpack on the kitchen table and sit down in a chair. I allow myself ten minutes of hyperventilating and worried thoughts, then I pull my books out of my bag and start on my homework. Three hours later, Jackie gets home from work as I'm putting away the last textbook back into my backpack.

"Hey, sweetie. Where's Chris?"

I shrug as I lift my backpack onto my shoulder and head for the stairs.

"You okay, Claire?" she calls after me.

"I'm fine. Thanks."

I race up the last few steps and close my bedroom door softly behind me. Collapsing onto my bed, I stare up at the blank ceiling and allow the first tears to fall. I can call or text him, but, for the first time in the two years we've been together, I don't think he'll respond.

I slide my phone out of my pocket and stare at the screen. I'm about to check for missed calls and texts, when the phone starts ringing. It's Chris.

"Hello?"

I can hear movement, but he doesn't answer.

"Chris?"

More movement, then I hear Tristan laughing.

He dialed my number on mistake.

I should hang up, but my curiosity gets the better of me. I listen for a few more seconds and Chris's voice makes my stomach ache again.

"She can sit with me."

"Aw... Is that your new girlfriend now that you're kicking Claire to the curb?"

"Fuck — " There's a loud rustling then the line goes dead.

I throw the phone across the room and the battery pops off when it hits the wall. Turning over onto my side, I curl up and close my eyes. Jackie will probably come up in a few minutes to call me down for dinner. But she'll leave me alone if she thinks I'm asleep. Then, when Chris comes home later, she'll tell him not to disturb me.

Just a few minutes later, Jackie knocks on the door. Then I hear the door squeak as she peeks inside. She softly closes the door and I let out the breath I was holding.

So Chris and Tristan are out with some girls and I'm lying here hiding from him and Jackie. What is wrong with me? I'm not going to lie back and take this.

I sit up and turn on the lamp on my bedside table. I retrieve my phone from the other side of the room, then I dial Chris's number. The call is immediately routed to voice-mail, but I don't bother leaving a message. I consider texting him, but decide against it. He probably turned his phone off when he realized he had accidentally called me.

I turn my phone off and drop it into the top drawer of my bedside table. Then I turn off the lamp, roll over and go to sleep.

I wake to the sound of Chris's voice. "Claire."

Opening my eyes, the room is pitch black, but the soft silver glow of the streetlights illuminates the left side of Chris's face as he kneels next to my bed.

"Go away."

"Claire, we need to talk."

"Why? So you can 'kick me to the curb'?"

"What are you talking about?"

"Get out!"

"Babe, just calm down."

I slide out of bed and he stands up. Immediately, I begin pushing him toward the door. "Get out. I don't want to hear what you have to say. I don't want to look at you. Just get out!"

"What the fuck! You're the one who couldn't answer one fucking question and you're pushing *me* out?"

"It was a stupid question!"

"You think it's stupid that I want to know about your relationships with other guys?"

"I don't have relationships with other guys!"

I keep pushing him until his back hits the inside of my closed bedroom door.

"Keep your voice down or my mom's gonna hear us."

"I don't care if she hears us arguing. I hope she does. And I hope they send me somewhere else where I don't have to hear your stupid voice."

He glares at me through the murky darkness and I can feel the rage building inside him with every heaving breath he takes. "That's what you want? You want to throw this all away without letting me explain a fucking thing? Fine. Have it your way."

He opens the door and slips out of my bedroom without another sound.

A jolt of blinding pain lights up my chest and I cover my face as I sink to my knees and double over. What have we done?

I look up at the door, half hoping it will open at any moment and Chris will appear to make this right. Instead, all I see is my backpack lying on the floor a few feet away. I crawl to it and hastily slide open the zipper. Then I yank out the crumpled drawing Jason gave me and I rip it up into at least twenty pieces and throw it in the trash.

three weeks later

I step onto the bus and trudge down the aisle to the usual seat in the back. Halfway down the aisle, I look up and my heart stops at the sight of Chris sitting in my usual row of seats. All the pain and misery of the past three weeks floods my veins at once and my breath hitches in my chest. I drag my feet forward until I reach his row and he hands me a folded piece of paper before he scoots over to make room for me.

I take the piece of paper from his hand and sit down next to him, positioning my backpack between us on the seat. I unfold the paper, which has clearly been taped together, and I'm not surprised to see the drawing I threw away in my bedroom three weeks ago. Chris has taped a post-it note with a word bubble saying, "I'm sorry," to the front of the picture.

But it's what's wrapped inside the drawing that makes me want to cry in the middle of a crowded bus. Two tickets to prom.

I didn't expect Chris to take me to my senior prom now that he's dropped out. But when we broke up three weeks ago, I knew that there was definitely no chance it would happen. I actually cried to Rachel about it last week when she asked me if Chris and I had gotten back together yet. I didn't expect her to tell Chris that I was sad about the prom.

And I didn't expect her to tell me the truth about what happened when Chris accidentally called me three weeks ago. Apparently, the girl he was going to sit with was Tristan's little sister Molly. And they were sitting together in Tristan's truck on the way to get frozen yogurt. Yes, I felt stupid. But that was six days ago and I still haven't figured out how to approach Chris.

He leans over to whisper something in my ear, but I honestly don't care what he has to say. I turn my face toward him and surprise him with a kiss on the cheek. His hands instantly reach up to cradle my face and I let out a deep sigh. How I've missed those hands.

I nuzzle my cheek into his palm and he smiles. I don't care if there are dozens of eyes on us right now.

He leans his forehead against mine. "Let's never break up again, okay?"

I nod and end up banging my forehead on his.

He laughs. "You don't have to get violent on me. I know I fucked up."

"We both did." I fold up the paper and the tickets and tuck them into my backpack.

"Don't lose those tickets," he warns me. "Or I'll have to go to the prom with Joanie Tipton."

"Ugh. Don't even joke about that."

"She was standing in line behind me when I went to buy these right now. Somehow she knew we were broken up and she offered to take me to the prom if you said no."

"Oh, my God. I hate her."

He rests his hand on my knee as the bus pulls out of the loading zone. "So do I."

I slide my hand under his palm, then I lace my fingers through his. And just like that, all is forgiven. Just like that, the world is turned right side up again.

FOREVER HAPPY

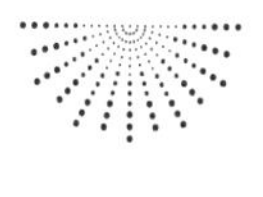

CHRIS

Tristan arrives at our house on the morning of Claire's senior prom in his shitty Ford pickup truck. Claire and I climb into the front seat with Tristan, with Claire between us. She leans her head on my shoulder and closes her eyes as the truck bumps along down the beltline. She's still tired from staying up late studying for finals.

We have to pick up Claire's dress and my outfit at the mall. This is totally last minute. Claire didn't want to pick up her dress on my bike, and Tristan's been putting this off every day for the last four days I've been asking him to take us. Claire's been too busy studying to care about Tristan blowing us off.

"What's the theme for the prom? White Trash Love?" Tristan remarks when he sees what I'm wearing to the prom.

I pay the girl at the cash register for my black Rolling Stones T-shirt and the new pair of jeans. The girl stares at my new mohawk hairdo and smiles. Claire hooks her arm around mine, staking her claim.

"You're just jealous you won't get to fly your white trash flag today," Claire says to Tristan.

"Yeah, not really. I wouldn't go to the prom if you paid me in white trash love."

"Hey," I reply, issuing a warning before Tristan and Claire start sniping at each other.

Ever since Tristan and Ashley broke up in the beginning of the school year, he's been an even bigger prick. He doesn't say stupid stuff that often, but when he does, it's usually something that's meant to make me jealous and hurt Claire at the same time.

I know he's just fucked up over Ashley, but it's been almost a year since they broke up and they were only together a year. And he still refuses to tell me why they broke up. He keeps giving me some lame story about how he broke up with her because he didn't have time to visit her after she went off to college. She's a year older than Tristan. I have a feeling Ashley's the one who broke up with him, and he still hasn't gotten over it. But he'll never admit that.

We leave the store and head for the department store where Claire had her dress altered. The center of the corridor in the mall is lined with craggily trees covered in blinking golden lights. Claire jumps up to touch one of the branches as we pass.

"These remind me of something," she says, looking back at the tree she just touched with a childlike smile lighting up her beautiful face.

"What do they remind you of?" I ask, grabbing her hand to get her attention.

"When I was a kid, before my mom died, we had this giant tree on our property. Sometimes, when my mom was really out of it, I'd go outside and climb the tree. I'd stay up there for hours sometimes, just looking up at the stars."

She continues to smile as she recalls this memory. And immediately my brain starts conjuring up ways to bring that kind of happiness to her every single day.

"Do you really think Jackie thinks you and Claire are just friends? Or even worse, like siblings? Ew!" Rachel has come over to help Claire with her hair and makeup. At least, that's the story Rachel and I are going with.

Claire can't respond with Rachel drawing a line around her lips, so I respond for both of us. "I don't know if she knows about us, but I doubt she'd say anything about it at this point. It's been... how long have we been together, babe?"

Claire pushes Rachel's hand away. "Almost two years!" She glares at me as if I should know this off the top of my head. "Anyway, she probably already knows, but we're still not going to officially tell her until I'm eighteen. Just to be safe."

Rachel grabs Claire's jaw so she can finish applying her makeup. "Well, you two better use protection tonight. Your mom's not stupid. I'm pretty sure your mom knows how to count up to nine months."

Claire doesn't correct Rachel or say anything about waiting until she's eighteen. It's nobody's business. Besides, her eighteenth birthday is only a few months away. Then I'm going to ravage her.

But tonight isn't about having sex. It's about giving Claire one memorable high school experience. An experience she thought she wouldn't get to have until I surprised her with some prom tickets two weeks ago. I guess I can bear a few hours with my old classmates if it will make Claire happy.

We leave the house just before six p.m. and Claire looks surprised, almost a little nervous, when she sees that Rachel is staying.

"I'm just gonna hang with Jackie for a while. She's teaching me to make protein bars for Jake," Rachel says, then she turns to me. "Hey, maybe I should leave some protein bars for you."

She tries to pinch my bicep and I step out of her reach. "Not funny."

My mom shakes her head. "Be nice to him, Rachel. Even if he does look like a juvenile delinquent tonight."

I smile as I run my hand over my mohawk, savoring the tickle of the spikes on my skin. "Don't give me that look. Claire's the one who made me dress like this."

"I did not! Stop lying!" Claire pushes me and I laugh.

"Oh, you two." My mom kisses Claire on the cheek, then she turns to me with a look of disgust and pats my arm. "Have fun, but don't come home too late. And no drunk driving!"

"I'll be drunk texting you later." I kiss her cheek and she rolls her eyes at me.

The black blazer I'm wearing over my Rolling Stones T-shirt gets us into the dance hall at the hotel, but I quickly peel it off once we're inside. I manage to make it through four and a half hours of pop music and corny ballads without puking. All I can think of as I dance with Claire or even as we're taking our prom pictures, is the surprise I have waiting for her at home.

FOREVER SURPRISED

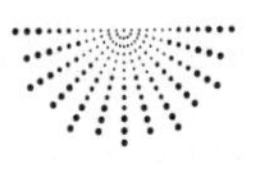

CLAIRE

Despite all the small hitches, prom night turns out to be even more magical than I imagined it would be. I don't care that Chris painted the tips of his mohawk blue. I don't care that he wore a T-shirt and jeans when all the other guys wore their dorky suits and tuxedos. I actually love that he looks so different than all these clones.

He's crazy, sexy, and beautiful. And he's all mine.

Shortly after we take our very memorable prom pictures, Chris and I decide it's time to go home. I'm exhausted from not having slept much this week. And I'm not a high-heels kind of girl. My feet are killing me.

Chris kills the engine on his motorcycle a couple of houses away from our house. Then he rolls the bike down the street, up the driveway, and into the garage while I walk next to him, carrying my heels in my hand.

"Thank you for making this one of the best nights of my life," I whisper as soon as we enter the house.

He smiles as he closes the front door and locks the deadbolt. "The night isn't over yet. I have a surprise for you in your room. Come on."

He grabs my hand and pulls me toward the stairs. I pull the front of the blazer tightly closed when I get a chill. Chris made me wear his coat on the bike for the ride home. But it smells so much like him, I don't want to take it off. I don't want this night to end.

"Close your eyes," he whispers when we get to my bedroom door, which is closed. I never leave my door shut unless I'm sleeping.

I close my eyes and bite my lip as I hear the soft click of the door opening and Chris pulls me inside.

"Okay, open your eyes."

I open my eyes and the room is completely dark. I'm confused, until Chris hits the light switch and the room is illuminated with a warm amber glow. On the wall next to my bed, strings of a few hundred, or even a thousand, lights have been pinned to the wall forming the brilliant, glowing silhouette of a craggily tree.

One tiny story about a tree and this is what Chris turns it into. Magic.

I coil my arms around his waist and lay my cheek against his shoulder. "It's so beautiful."

He kisses the top of my head. "There are some stars on the ceiling too, but they're glow-in-the-dark. You have to expose them to light for a while, then turn off the lights and they'll glow. And you can watch the stars any time you want."

"I don't know how you even thought to do this and how much you had to pay Rachel to go along with it, but you are ... you're my knight in shining armor. I mean, this is like a damn fairy tale."

He grabs my face and tips my head back so he can look me in the eye. "I'll do anything to make you happy."

I clutch the front of his T-shirt as he plants a soft kiss on my lips.

"You know what would make me very happy right now?"

He kisses the tip of my nose and smiles. "What?"

"If you slept with me in my bed tonight."

He gazes into my eyes, not blinking or smiling. I know he's thinking of what will happen if Jackie catches us sleeping in my room, but I don't care.

"Please. You know I haven't slept much this week. I don't think I'll be able to fall asleep after a night like this. Not without you next to me."

Finally, he smiles. "I'll sing you to sleep."

I let him watch as I change into my pajamas, even though I can see his chest heaving. I know I'm testing our boundaries, but it just feels right tonight. Chris, on the other hand, removes his T-shirt but refuses to get out of his jeans. He doesn't trust himself.

I scoot in under the covers of my twin bed until I'm up against the wall with the glowing tree next to me. Chris scoots in next to me and I immediately lay my head on his shoulder as he wraps his arm around me.

"What do you want me to sing?"

"Whatever you want to sing."

He clears his throat and takes a deep breath before he begins singing a song I've never heard before, but it's beautiful. It must be one of those classic rock songs he loves. I only remember a few of them from the rare times when my mom was sober and she'd turn on the radio to clean the house.

When he starts singing the chorus it sounds a little more familiar, but I still can't put my finger on it. As if he can sense my confusion, he stops singing.

"Do you know what song this is?"

"No... Sorry."

"You've never heard 'Your Song' by Elton John?"

I shrug. "I don't think so."

He sighs so loudly it's almost a groan. "I'll teach you this song. It's one of his best songs. You have to learn it."

"Why do *I* have to learn it?"

"Because you love me and I want you to sing it with me."

I shake my head. "No. I don't sing. That's your job."

"I'll have you singing like an angel in no time."

He sings the song again from the beginning, as I rest my hand on his bare chest. Halfway through the song, he grabs my hand and laces his fingers through mine. I glance over my shoulder once more at the twinkling tree on the wall behind me. Then I close my eyes and drift off.

FOREVER FRUSTRATED

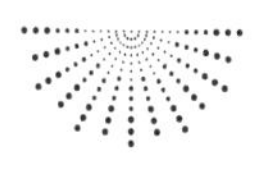

CHRIS

AUGUST 9, 2011

I toss the empty Capri-Sun pouch into the waste bin under the kitchen sink, then I gaze at Claire across the breakfast bar. She's sitting cross-legged on the barstool. Claire is the only person I've ever known who sits cross-legged on barstools. It's one of the quirks I love most about her.

"What are you grinning at?" she says as she looks up from the magazine she's reading.

"Why do you read that shit? None of those girls are as beautiful as you."

"I read it for the articles."

I round the breakfast bar and wrap my arms around her waist. "I know a few articles I'd like to get rid of today," I say, burying my face in her neck. "Happy birthday, babe."

"What if your mom walks in?" She pries my arms off her and pushes me back.

"She just left to the shop. She won't be back for at least three hours. Come upstairs with me." I spin the barstool around so she's facing me. "I want to give you your birthday present."

She narrows her eyes at me, but she can't hide the smile that curls the corners of her perfect lips. Grabbing the front of my shirt, she pulls me toward her.

Her lips hover over mine. "Only if you promise not to sing the birthday song."

I laugh as I plant a quick kiss on her lips. "Asking me not to sing to you on your birthday is like asking me not to breathe." I grab her hand and pull her off the stool. "Come on."

She follows me upstairs to her bedroom. When we get there, she starts tidying up, putting away clothes and straightening the pictures of us she has tucked in the frame of her mirror. I come up behind her and press my body against hers as I reach for a picture of us. I slip the picture out of the mirror frame and hold it in front of her face.

It's a picture of us in front of a hot dog stand at the blues festival where Claire and I had our first kiss. I asked the hot dog vendor to take the picture with her new phone. It was so hot that summer, and she was wearing these tiny cutoff shorts. It was so hard not to touch her as the guys took the picture, but I knew we couldn't have any photographic evidence of our relationship. All the secrecy ends today.

I hold the picture up in front of her face as I kiss the back of her neck. "This was one of my favorite days. Because this is the day you told me you loved me."

She spins around in my arms and flashes me a warm smile. "Yeah, but I loved you long before that."

I toss the picture onto the floor and grab the back of her neck as I slowly bring my lips to hers. I kiss her slowly as she clutches the front of my shirt for support. Her tongue brushes against mine and I instantly get hard.

"Fuck," I whisper, pulling her toward the bed to lay her down.

She wraps her arms around my neck and she's still smiling as I gently lie down on top of her. Placing one of my legs between hers, I slowly slide her legs open. Then I slip my hand under her shirt and her skin prickles with goose bumps.

She's so fucking soft. I slide my hand farther up and her body goes rigid.

"I love you," I whisper against her lips and she immediately pushes me off.

I sigh and try not to curse as I lie back next to her.

"I'm sorry," she says, staring at the ceiling. "I'm just scared that it's going to hurt and then I'll feel different about you. I don't want to feel like you've hurt me."

I flip onto my side and nuzzle my nose in her hair, inhaling the floral scent of her shampoo. She smells like a warm summer breeze. Her breathing quickens when my lips graze her ear. I lay a soft kiss on her cheekbone and slip my hand under her shirt again, eager to feel her skin.

I'm pretty good at knowing what Claire likes. And just how far I can go with her. Her body will tell me if she's ready.

I trace my finger around her navel and she smiles as she arches her back a little.

"I could never hurt you.... But I can't fucking lie. I want to be inside you so bad." I continue tracing a light circle, imagining my fingers between her legs and this erection is getting unbearable. "I want to make you feel as good as you make me feel." I lift her shirt a few inches and lay a soft kiss on her belly. Her skin is warm against my lips. I want her so bad. "But I'll wait as long as it takes."

She brushes my hair out of my face as my lips hover over her navel. "I love you," she whispers.

This is it. Today is the day.

I scoot up and plant a quick kiss on her temple before I spring off the bed. "I'll be right back, babe." Then I leave to get my guitar.

FOREVER YOURS

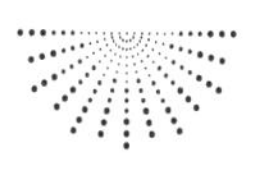

CLAIRE

Chris's lips smell and taste like the berry Capri-Sun he was just sipping and I can't shake the feeling that we're too young to be alone in my room. But it feels so right as his fingers lightly graze my ribs sending chills through every part of my body. I'm eighteen today. Eighteen is a perfectly fine age to lose your virginity; especially if it's with the boyfriend you've been with for more than two years, who also happens to be the most amazing, patient boyfriend a girl could ask for.

His hand slides farther up and I flinch when his fingers hit the wire of my bra. "I love you."

He whispers these words he's uttered a million times. Words that always seem to soothe me. Today, they have the opposite effect. Instead of putting me at ease, I feel completely on edge. My entire body buzzing with nerves.

I push him off and he sighs as he lies back. "I'm sorry," I mutter, totally aware that I shouldn't have to apologize about not feeling ready.

But I have to take into account how patient Chris has been the past two years. And I'm not an idiot. I start college next week and he's going to be playing a lot more gigs now that the band has a legit manager. He's going to have girls screaming his name; ready and willing to spread their legs for him whenever he wants. I know it's up to Chris to resist temptation, but how can I expect him to resist if I keep rejecting him.

"I'm just scared that it's going to hurt and then I'll feel different about you. I don't want to feel like you've hurt me."

He turns onto his side and buries his nose in my hair, breathing in the scent of the shampoo he loves so much. The sensation of his face in my hair gives me the chills. I want him. I do. I just wish I wasn't so scared.

He kisses my cheek, then he slips his hand under my T-shirt and traces circles around my belly button. "I could never hurt you ... But I can't fucking lie. I want to be inside you so bad ... I want to make you feel as good as you make me feel." He plants a soft kiss on my belly and I shiver. "But I'll wait as long as it takes."

I run my fingers through his hair as I brush it out of his face. "I love you."

He plants a quick kiss on my temple before he springs off

the bed, leaving me feeling a little used up. "I'll be right back, babe."

I swallow hard as I look up at the glow-in-the-dark stars stuck to the ceiling. I glance at the strings of lights on the wall next to me in the shape of a tree. I think of my mom.

I don't know how she got pregnant or who my father was — is. All I know is that my mom was alone for the brief time I spent with her. She didn't trust men, which makes me wonder if she even knew my father.

What I do know is that Chris is not the type to leave if things should get complicated. I know no birth control is one hundred percent effective. But I have nothing to worry about. If I were to get pregnant, I know Chris would be there for me every step of the way.

Chris comes back a minute later with his acoustic guitar and closes the bedroom door behind him. No one else is home. Jackie and her new boyfriend Tim are baking a cake at the shop and running errands before we meet them tonight for a birthday dinner. Which is where Chris and I will finally confess the truth about our relationship.

This simple gesture of Chris closing the bedroom door makes me feel safe, like he knows exactly what I need. He always has.

I scoot back so he can sit on the edge of the bed next to me. He settles down with his guitar in his lap and strums a haphazard melody as he tunes the guitar by ear. I sigh as I watch his lips playing with the ball piercing in his tongue.

He presses the tip of his tongue against the back of his bottom teeth and pushes the piercing forward just far enough to catch it between his teeth. Then the tip of his tongue flicks up to touch the ball just as it retreats. He does this over and over and I'm convinced that he knows how erotic it looks, though he claims it's unintentional.

"I wrote this for you," he begins, looking more than a bit nervous. "It's about the day we met. It's called 'Sleepyhead'."

I smile as I remember how tired I was the day we met. I hadn't slept at all the night before at the police station, but somehow he still convinced me to go downstairs and listen to him play. Chris has always had a way of making me feel comfortable while doing something completely out of my comfort zone.

He begins plucking the guitar strings and the melody that flows out is both haunting and sweet. I'm already on the verge of tears from the memory of the day we met when he begins to sing.

"Feels so wrong to want this. You look so broken there. A flicker in the mist, as tired as the air." He looks up at me and my breath hitches. He holds my gaze the entire time he's singing, except when he closes his eyes and belts out the chorus. "So frightened of the dark. You're my sleepyhead.

Hiding with the stars. Put your dreams to bed, my sleepyhead."

I grab his face and kiss him hard. He slides the guitar off his lap and onto the floor, then he climbs on top of me. I wrap my legs around him and he moans as I grind my hips into him.

"Are you okay?" he murmurs into my mouth.

I nod as I wrap my arms tighter around his solid shoulders and mash my lips to his. His hand slips under my shirt and I suck in a sharp breath as it travels up to my breast. Chris and I have gone much further than this, hundreds of times, but this feels different. I want him to see all of me.

I push his shoulders back a little so I can reach down and lift my shirt over my head. He smiles and does the same. I sit up so he can get a better look at me.

His eyes are glued to my breasts for a moment. Then he looks up and the devilish smile on his face could set this house on fire. I reach forward and lightly drag my fingertips down the center of his chest until I reach the button of his jeans. His nostrils flare as his chest heaves with anticipation.

I unbutton his jeans and slowly slide the zipper down. His erection is ready to burst out, and suddenly I'm dying to see it.

I swallow hard as I look up into his eyes. "I want to see it."

He chuckles, then he slides off the bed and slowly strips

off his jeans and boxers so he's completely naked. He's so beautiful. This is what I've been missing out on.

I stand from the bed and shrug out of my shorts and panties. Then I turn my back to him so he can undo my bra. His fingers work gently, undoing the clasp, then he slowly slides the straps down my arms and we let it fall to the floor.

I turn around to face him and he looks stunned, as if he didn't think he'd ever get here. I take his face in my hands and try not to giggle when his erection prods my belly.

"Sorry," he whispers.

"It's okay. Did that hurt?"

He smiles and shakes his head. "No. Definitely not."

His gaze keeps falling to my breasts. I lay myself down on the bed and grab his hand to pull him down next to me.

"I just want to kiss you … everywhere," he says, his hand reaching for my waist.

He pulls my body flush against his, and this time his erection slides between my legs. He leans in to kiss me and I drape my leg over his hips. My body gets warm and pliable as he moves his hips slowly, rubbing himself against me.

But he quickly stops and lifts my leg off of him. "We can't do that or I'm gonna blow."

He reaches over the side of the bed and lifts his jeans off the floor. He pulls out a condom from his wallet and I watch as he pinches the reservoir and slides it over his erection. Just the way we learned how to do it in sex ed class. I try not to picture him doing that with the girls he was with before me.

He lies next to me, propped up on one elbow as his gaze slides over every inch of my skin. "I am so fucking fascinated by your body." He traces his finger lightly over the inside of my thigh until he reaches my center. I gasp as his finger easily slides over my flesh, finding the most sensitive spot. "I just want to look at you for a while. Is that okay?"

"Yes," I whisper, breathless with anticipation.

He removes his hand from between my legs and lays it flat on my belly. Then he slowly slides his hand up to my breast, at the same time pushing me onto my back. He cups my breast in his hand and watches my face as he gently rolls my nipple between his thumb and forefinger. I smile as both my nipples perk up and the pulsing sensation between my legs returns.

He leans over, his eyes locked on mine, as he flicks my nipple with his tongue. Each time, it sends a rush of excitement coursing through me. Then he closes his eyes as he takes my nipple into his mouth and sucks gently.

I let out a soft whimper and draw in a deep breath. He releases my nipple and lays a cool trail of kisses down my stomach, stopping when he gets to my navel. I glance down to see what he's doing and he's just staring at me. I open my mouth to say something, but he plants a soft kiss on the inside of my thigh.

With one hand, he parts my flesh and I gasp as he uses the fingers of his other hand to softly caress me. He uses two fingers, rubbing me in a gentle up-and-down motion. My stomach muscles contract and I can hardly breathe.

"Oh, my God."

He leans over and plants a tender kiss on me, holding his mouth there so I can feel his breath on my bare skin. Then his tongue makes contact with my clit. It's just a soft lick, but I feel as if I might burst.

"You taste so fucking good," he murmurs against my skin.

Then he licks me again and again.

I grab fistfuls of the comforter and arch my back. "Oh, God!"

He takes my clit into his mouth and sucks gently until my body begins to convulse uncontrollably. *Oh, my God. This is so embarrassing.* But he doesn't seem to care. He continues to devour me until I let out a wild scream. Then I grab his hair and yank him up so I can catch my breath.

He smiles as he hovers above me, his elbows resting on the pillow on either side of my head. "Was that good?" I nod because I still can't speak. "Are you ready or do you need a minute?"

I nod again. "I'm ready."

He kisses my forehead and I take a few deep breaths. His

hand slides down between us and I spread my legs a little wider. Then I hold my breath and brace myself.

The tip of his erection glides between my flesh as he searches for entry. I jump a little when he hits my sensitive clit. Then he finds what he's looking for and I dig my fingernails into his shoulders as he slowly slides into me just an inch.

He squeezes his eyes tightly shut. "God damn."

"Are you okay?"

He nods emphatically. "Oh, yeah. I'm very okay."

He opens his eyes and leans down to kiss me as he attempts to slide in farther. I can taste myself on his lips and it makes me smile. Then he tries to slide in farther and I yelp.

"Shit! Did I hurt you?"

"No, no, no! It's okay." I grab his face and kiss him again. "Just go slow. Please."

I suck on his top lip and he groans as he slides just a bit farther in with each stroke. I can feel my muscles and flesh stretching with every movement of his hips. He bobs slowly up and down, back and forth, grinding against me in a circular motion, then resting so he can kiss me deeply. It feels like it goes on for an hour, but in reality it's more like ten minutes before he lets go inside the condom and collapses on top of me.

I lay a soft kiss on his sweaty forehead as I brush the hair out of his face. I can feel him softening inside me, then he reaches down and carefully pulls himself out.

"I'll be right back."

When he returns from the bathroom, he's still naked and that makes me smile. He slides in under the covers with me and we just lie facing each other without saying anything for a while. He strokes the backs of his fingers over my cheekbone and plants a tender kiss on my nose.

"I love you so much, Claire." He brushes his thumb across my lips. "I want you to be with me forever."

I swallow the lump in my throat and gaze into his eyes. "Forever yours."

He rests his hand over my heart. "Forever mine."

I place my hand on his chest. "Forever ours."

FOREVER STARTING OVER

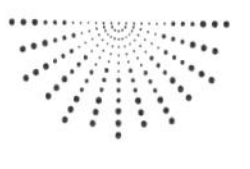

CLAIRE

I open my desk drawer and consider taking my old hairbrush, so I'll have two: the new one and the old one. But then I have a sobering thought. Going off to college is a new experience. It shouldn't be encumbered by old things. Right?

Chris pulls my hand away from the desk and pushes the drawer closed. "That's enough. You've checked all your drawers four times. I think it's safe to say you didn't forget anything."

The butterflies in my stomach spread over my entire body, until I feel as if my skin is humming with nervous energy.

He turns me around to face him and takes my hands in his. "Are you ready?"

I shake my head. "I'm so nervous."

"It will be fine. And you can call me if it gets really bad. I'll be there in thirty minutes."

I take a deep breath as I look around the room. It looks almost exactly the same as it did before I packed. I didn't want to bring too many things with me to the dorm. I want this room to still feel like home whenever I visit.

"Are you still playing that gig tonight?" I ask, hoping he'll tell me it was canceled.

He nods his head. "Couldn't get out of it. Xander said this guy has a lot of pull with Arista Records. If I play a few more shows there, and they do well, he might pull some strings for me."

"That's good."

I don't mention how this means I can't call him if I get really homesick tonight. I can only call him on the nights when he doesn't have a show.

Jackie walks in and lets out a deep sigh as she tilts her head. "It won't be the same without you here."

"Stop pretending, Mom. You were just telling me how happy you'll be when Claire is gone so you can finally win Dance Dance Revolution."

"Stop it, Christopher. That's not funny," she chides him, but I try not to laugh.

I let go of Chris's hands and turn to Jackie so I can give her a hug. She squeezes me so tight. I'm almost afraid to pull away. I'm afraid she's crying. I've never seen Jackie cry. I don't think I'd be able to handle that.

When we finally let go of each other, her eyes are pink and watery, but she blinks a few times and the moment is gone. She wipes a few tears from my jaw and smiles.

"I fully expect you to spend at least one weekend here every month. Chris will pick you up. You're only forty minutes away."

"I'll try my hardest."

"I know." She kisses my forehead and gives me another quick hug. "Get out of here before I start crying. Go."

Chris and I chuckle as we leave Jackie in my bedroom.

"Go. Get out of here," Chris says, tapping my butt to push me toward the stairs.

"Stop!" I laugh, smacking his hand away.

Chris drives me to the dorm in Jackie's car. I spend most of the drive there hugging my knees to my chest to comfort myself. When he pulls into the parking lot at Spencer Hall, I get even more nervous as I wonder who I'm rooming with.

Chris parks in the loading zone and grabs my two boxes out of the trunk while I take my purse and my suitcase. I have my card-key, but a girl with curly hair and square glasses is nice enough to hold the door open for us to enter.

"Thanks," I say.

I hope my roommate is someone like that. *Please let me get a nice roommate.*

We get off the elevator on the second floor and head for room 207. Chris sets the boxes down next to the door and I knock. I can hear footsteps on the other side of the door. My roommate is already here.

The door opens and a tall girl with beautiful dark hair and golden skin flashes me a tight smile. "Hi," she says softly.

"Hi. I'm Claire. I think you're my roommate." I grab the piece of paper that's folded and tucked in my back pocket, which shows my dorm assignment.

Before I can unfold the paper, she opens the door wide for us. Chris and I come in with my stuff and I see she's already taken the bed on the left, closest to the door. Her bed is covered in a gray and lavender comforter. But, other than a few bottles of lotion and hairspray, the desk on her side of the room is pretty bare. No dozens of pictures of friends and family.

Chris places my boxes on my new bed and looks around. "This place could use a little love."

He wiggles his eyebrows at me and I shake my head as I turn to my new roommate. "I'm sorry. I don't think I got your name."

"Senia," she replies, plopping down on her bed. "Short for Yesenia."

"That's pretty." I look at Chris and he raises his eyebrows. This girl obviously is not in the mood to talk.

"You want me to help you unpack," he asks, grabbing my hand to pull me against him.

I press my hands against his chest, unsure whether we should be affectionate in front of Senia. It might make her uncomfortable. He smiles when he notices what I'm doing, then he leans in to try and kiss me.

"Stop," I whisper, but he just laughs. "I can unpack by myself. Are you leaving now?"

"Trying to get rid of me already?"

I try to transmit the answer to that question telepathically, so Senia can't hear how desperately I don't want him to leave yet.

"I have to go move the car and get ready for the show," he says. I guess he didn't receive my telepathic message. "Do you need anything before I go?"

I shake my head. "Call me before the show ... to say goodnight." I whisper the last three words so my new roommate can't hear how needy I'm feeling right now.

He smiles and kisses my forehead. "I will. I love you, babe."

"I love you."

I wrap my arms around his waist and breathe in as much of his scent as I can before he leaves. I close the door behind him and Senia is looking at me when I turn around.

"Is that your boyfriend?" she asks.

"Yeah. I'm sorry. I didn't introduce you two. His name is Chris." I move the boxes off my bed and onto the floor.

"Is he some kind of actor or something? He said he had to get ready for a show."

I laugh as I lift the suitcase onto my bed. "No, he's a musician. He has a band. They're playing a show tonight."

"Oh." She keeps playing with her phone for a moment, then she looks up from the screen with a sober expression on her face. "My dad wouldn't let me date anyone when I was in high school."

"Sorry," I reply, unsure what else to say to that.

She shrugs and flashes me a smile. "It's okay. I think this year is going to be different. You know?"

I let out an uneasy chuckle. "Yeah, I do."

FOREVER PLAYING

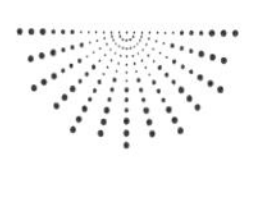

CHRIS

The text I just received from Claire says that she and Senia just got here to The Pinhook club in Durham. I text her back to let her know we're still setting up, then I slide my phone into my back pocket. Tristan is helping Jake set up the drums while I do a quick sound check on my guitar. The floor is already packed with so many people, I can hardly hear myself think. My eyes scan the crowd, searching for Claire's blonde hair as I test each guitar string. Everywhere I look I see Duke, UNC, and NC State T-shirts. Reminders of all the studying that's been keeping me from Claire for the past five weeks since she moved into the dorm.

A few minutes later, I'm adjusting the mic stand when I spot Claire's blonde ponytail bouncing across the front of the club near the bar. I finish setting up the microphone, then I tap the head. The chatter in the crowd is suddenly replaced by screaming and a few wolf whistles. I flash one of the whistlers near the stage my *crowd smile* and she blows me a kiss.

I wet my lips, then I look out across floor to where Claire is making her way toward the stage. "How's everyone doing tonight?"

The collective roar of two hundred people shouting two hundred different answers to that question is ridiculous, but it gets me pumped. I love playing to an enthusiastic crowd. My eyes lock on Claire as she tries to squeeze past a guy in a newsboy cap. He gives her an angry look, like she's crazy if she thinks she's getting past him.

"Hey, you," I say, pointing at the guy in the cap. "Let the girl through. She's a special guest."

The guy rolls his eyes as he lets Claire and Senia to scoot past him so they can get right up next to the stage. Claire shakes her head as I wink at her, but Senia's too busy hugging her drink to her chest to keep it from spilling to acknowledge me.

Tristan is still setting up his bass, so I decide to engage the crowd while we wait. "We may be waiting a while, so I'm gonna tell you all a little story. Do any of you know who Neil Hardaway is?" About two-thirds of the crowd answers affirmatively, which isn't surprising since he a blues legend in the

Carolina music scene. "Well, when I was about eleven, I sent Neil Hardaway a letter asking if he could send me the tabs for his song 'Greensboro Blues.' I never received a reply, so I figured he was just too busy to send them to me himself. So I sent another letter to the same address, but this letter was addressed to 'Neil Hardaway's Assistant.' I was certain that one would get a response." Claire smiles and shakes her head. She's heard this story before. "Well, I didn't get a response to that letter either. So a couple of years later, I had a brilliant idea, and I decided I'd try again. This time, I addressed the letter to Neil Hardaway and I included a picture of me dressed up as Neil, in a blue suit and black tie, electric guitar slung across my chest, a cigarette hanging out the corner of my mouth. And I signed the letter 'Future Neil Hardaway. If you don't send me the tabs, I can't go back in time to 1991 and write this song.' I got the tabs in the mail four days later."

After a brief moment of laughter, I glance at Tristan and he nods. I count to three and we go right into a hard-hitting rendition of one of our earliest tracks, "Justified." During the first song, Senia convinces a guy standing behind her to get her a few drinks. I can see Claire trying to talk some sense into her as Senia places her three drinks on the floor next to her feet, but Senia is not hearing it. She's hell-bent on getting shit-faced tonight.

When the second song is over, I decide to have a little

fun and play the first few notes of a song Tristan and I made up a few months ago called "Easy Fuck." It's not something we would ever play for a crowd, but just plucking out the first few notes makes Tristan roar with laughter as he watches Senia pick up a glass from the floor and chug it. Having made my point, we continue onto the third song of the night.

Halfway through the set, Senia is crossing her legs and fidgeting as if she has to piss. But she never goes to the restroom. She just keeps staring at Tristan with a dreamy look on her face. There's no way this is going to end well.

"We're gonna slow it down a little for the last song of the night. This is called 'First I Saw You.'" When the song is over, I thank everyone for coming and the frenzied cheers from the crowd are exactly what I came for. I take a bow while Tristan comes up behind me and pretends to grab my hips. I roll my eyes back and moan like I'm having an orgasm. Then we all take another bow and say goodnight.

Claire's eyes are narrowed at me as I hop off the stage into the crowd. But all is forgiven when I grab her by the back of the neck and kiss her. Her lips taste like iced tea. The flavor combined with the sound of the girls around us mumbling their disappointment gets me hot. I slide my tongue into her mouth and she whimpers as she grabs fist-fuls of my T-shirt.

I move down to kiss her neck and she pushes me back. "Okay, okay. That's enough."

I laugh as I plant a kiss on her cheek. "It's *never* enough."

FOREVER PROMISED

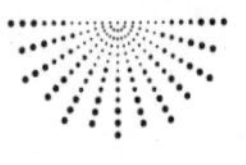

CHRIS

After we had sex two months ago, I knew I had to do something to show my commitment to Claire. Something to keep me in her mind when all those sex-starved college guys are trying to get a piece of her.

We're too young to get married — at least, according to Claire we are. But I hope this promise ring will serve as a little reminder of who she belongs to.

She swears that she hasn't had a lot of guys hitting on her, but she doesn't understand her own appeal. Claire doesn't ooze sex appeal until you know her. Before you know her, she exudes this closed-off, innocent vibe that begs to be explored. You can't help but want to get close to her; know more about her.

I'll admit that this aspect of her personality was a huge turn-on for me when she first walked into our living room four years ago. Now, it's just scary. I don't want anyone to take Claire away from me. But, most of all, I don't want anyone to hurt her.

I worry about her every day.

Claire sits down on the grass under a large oak tree in Moore Square. I sit next to her and lay my guitar on the grass next to me. She crosses her legs and sits up straight, like she's about to start meditating. We look around for a while at the groups of people enjoying a Saturday in the park on a long Columbus Day weekend. Forty feet away, a father is kneeling on the grass, playing catch with his toddler son and it gives me an idea.

"We're gonna have kids someday, right?"

She laughs. "Not for at least five or six years. But, yeah, I guess."

"We can't do it when we're old. I don't want to be one of those old parents who doesn't have energy to go to the park."

"Twenty-five is not that old."

"So ... if we're having kids in five or six years, when are we getting married?"

She's silent for a moment, then she turns to me with a question in her eyes. "What are you getting at?"

"Nothing. Just talking."

She scrunches her eyebrows together as if she doesn't believe me. "I don't know. After I graduate?"

"Why do we have to wait till then? I mean, it's not like we haven't already lived together. We could get married before you graduate, then move in together right after graduation."

"What are you saying? You want to get married now?"

"No, not now. Maybe your senior year or something." I shrug, suddenly regretting I brought this up. "Anyway, it's not a big deal. We can get married whenever. Or not. We don't have to ever get married."

"Now you don't want to get married?"

"That's not what I meant. I mean that we don't have to ever get married if you don't want to. We could be one of those progressive couples that stays together forever but never gets married because we're too cool for that."

"Sounds like an excuse not to get married," she says, leaning back on her hands and closing her eyes as she leans her head back.

I take the opportunity to take the promise ring out of my pocket. Then I lay the ring on her knee. She opens her eyes and stares at the ring for a while.

"What is that?"

"It's a ring." She glares at me and I laugh. "It's a promise ring."

She picks it up and examines it. "What kind of promise are we making?"

"I'm promising to love you forever. You can decide what kind of promise you want to make."

She smiles and looks me in the eye. Then she hands the ring back. "Aren't you supposed to put it on me?"

I take the ring from her, then I take her left hand in mine and slide it onto her middle finger. I lay a soft kiss on the back of her hand and look her in the eye.

"I promise to love you forever. Even when I'm lying in my grave, all dusty and cobwebbed. I'll be whispering your name inside my coffin."

"That is so creepy."

"Creepy and romantic."

She shakes her head and holds up her hand to look at the ring. Finally, she turns to me and places her hand on my cheek. "I promise to love you forever, *and* — "

"There's an *and?"*

"And ... I promise to make sure they bury me next to you so you can still sing me to sleep when we're dead."

"Now *that* is romantic."

She smiles, looking very impressed with herself. I lean over to plant a kiss on her cheek and she throws her arms around my neck. I lose my balance and fall backward. She lands on top of me and plants a kiss on my mouth. I grab her face before she can sit up again and lick her cheek.

"Ew!" She pushes off me and I laugh as we both sit up.

She straightens her shirt as she sits up straight and I lean in to whisper in her ear. "I'll settle for your cheek, but I'd rather lick you in other places."

She shakes her head, but I can see her brain working. Probably trying to think of a way to cut this outing short so we can go back to her bedroom or her dorm and lick each other. Not that I would object.

But first, I have a song I want to sing. What can I say? It's the performer in me.

I grab the guitar and begin playing an upbeat sort of bubble-gum pop song I've been working on since the day Claire first gave herself to me. I don't normally write that type of music, but I was on a bit of a high after that day. It seemed appropriate.

Claire spins around on the grass so she's facing me and I begin the first verse.

"Sun in your hair, ignites my insides,
Glow of your skin, lights me up right,
Touch of your hand, I'm on my knees here,
Begging please, baby, just stay near,
Yeah, right here.

'Cause we don't have to go nowhere,
This place is ours, it's everywhere,

Yeah, we can stay,
Stay forever.
Ours.
It'll stay forever ours."

I'm about to start the second verse when she gasps. "Forever Ours? Is that the name of the song?"

I place my hand over the strings of my guitar to stop the resonant sound. "Yeah, why?"

Her eyes widen as she smiles. "I got you something. This is so funny."

She reaches into the back pocket of her jeans and pulls out a smooth glass heart about half the size of my palm. She hands it to me and waits impatiently as I read the words engraved on the heart: *Ever thine, ever mine, ever ours.*

"I got it at a little stationery shop off campus."

I chuckle as I realize what I said to her two months ago stuck in her head, too. "Thank you," I say, then I kiss the corner of her mouth. "It's perfect."

She smiles and taps my guitar. "Sorry, I interrupted you. Can you finish the song now?"

I start the song from the beginning again, and by the second verse, a crowd of about six people have gathered around to listen. When the song is over, the crowd has grown to at least a dozen. They clap loudly and one man asks if I have a change bucket, but I tell him that's not necessary.

"Another one," Claire insists and the crowd joins in her plea.

I get the feeling I always get when I step onto a stage; that mixture of nervousness and excitement. That rush that I can't get enough of. And I slip right into another upbeat song.

After four songs, I have to quit. The crowd is getting too thick and I don't have a stage here to separate us. The last thing I need is for Claire and I to get crushed on the day I promise to love her until the day I die.

I give my appreciation to the crowd and say my good-byes. A few people ask for my name so they can look for my album, but I have to tell them I'm not signed yet. Still feels good to be asked.

"Where are we going?" I ask as Claire and I walk back to my bike.

"I don't care. Wherever you go, I go."

FOREVER STUDYING

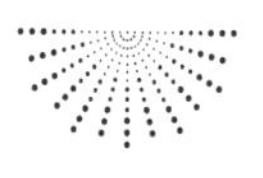

CLAIRE

Senia and I went to our first college party last week. And she met a boy. A very handsome, very strong football player. Tar-Heel running back Justin Neely. I think the only way to get Senia to come out of her shell may be to ply her with alcohol.

Of course, I don't drink. I never have. After losing my mother to a heroin overdose, I swore I'd never drink or do drugs. And I really have no desire to break that promise to myself.

But I must admit that it was fun to see Senia finally let loose a little. I wasn't aware just how shy she was until she opened up to me the second week of school. I had just asked her if she wanted to go get something to eat at the campus café and she rejected me.

I didn't think anything of it; though I was a bit disappointed. I've never really had any girlfriends, unless you count Rachel. But we only attended high school together for three weeks before she graduated. She's always seemed a little annoyed by my immaturity.

I thought Senia would finally be my chance at having a normal female friendship, but she didn't seem interested. So I grabbed some cash out of my wallet and I was all set to go to the café alone. Then Senia stopped me.

She opened up to me about how she only had a couple of friends in high school, but they went to a different school. And they weren't even good friends because her dad refused to let her go out partying or even to the mall or the movies. By the end of our discussion, I was beginning to think I had it good as a foster child.

So I gave her some time to loosen up a little, then we went to our first party last week. Neither of us are huge partiers, so we kept to ourselves most of the night. Until handsome Justin Neely approached shy little Senia and offered her a bottle of beer.

If it had been a cup, I would have made her reject the drink. But Justin opened the bottle right there in front of us, as if he knows the rules of staying safe at a college party. Never accept a drink from a stranger. Unless it's an unopened beverage.

One beer led to two tequila shots. Which led to another beer. Which led to me practically carrying her back to the dorm. And she's been babbling about Justin for eight days straight.

"He's taking me to meet his sister today," Senia says while brushing her dark, luxurious hair.

"Wow. Sounds serious. Do you mind if I make your bed?"

"Go ahead. Is Chris coming over?"

I smile in response. It's really all I can do. I haven't seen Chris in six days, but it seems like an eternity. I'm giddy with excitement.

Today, Chris and I aren't going to stay in the dorm and have sex for hours. Not that I object to that. But I was thinking we could get out for a change.

I know we're way past the dating phase of our relationship, but four months of weekends filled with almost nothing but sex and breakfast food feels almost wrong. Almost. I mean, we went to Moore Square a couple of months ago and that was beautiful.

And it's so cold outside. I thought we'd go get some coffee. Or something that normal couples do.

Then again, Chris is the only guy I've ever really been with. I'm not sure I know what normal couples do. They'd probably envy us.

Senia twists her hair and pins up one side of her hair. "How do I look?"

She's wearing a killer red dress she ordered online from an independent designer, accentuated by red lipstick.

"You look stunning."

"Really?"

"Really."

She sighs with relief. "Oh, my God, Claire. I think I'm in love."

"After one week?"

"Is that stupid?"

I smile, but I shake my head. "Not at all. I think I fell in love with Chris the moment I saw him."

Her phone rings and she grabs it off the desk. "Hello? … I'll be right out." She turns to me as she tucks the phone into her purse, looking slightly panicked. "He's here. I'll see you later. What time is a good time to come back?"

"Anytime you want. Chris and I are going out tonight."

"Really?"

"Yep."

She looks a little conflicted. "Is it a special occasion?"

"Nope. Just trying something different for a change."

She still looks confused. "But you guys stay in because you hardly ever see each other," she says, as if I don't know this. "If I were with him, I'd be staying in every night."

"What?"

"Oops. I'm not supposed to say stuff like that, am I? Sorry."

I laugh as I finish making my bed. "Good luck meeting the family."

"Thanks."

Twenty minutes later, I hear a knock at the door and I jump up from the bed. I grab my purse off the nightstand and drop my phone in. Then I open the door.

Chris is standing with his hands behind his back, looking down at me with that half-smile he flashes when he's on stage. His crowd smile. It's ridiculously hot and I hate that he's using it on me.

"Wanna study?" he asks in his sexiest voice.

Study is Chris's code word for oral sex. Chris may not be in school, but he's been doing a lot of studying lately. And it's as if my body has been conditioned to respond to this word. Whenever anyone mentions the word *study,* I get an ache between my legs.

Oh, who am I kidding. Senia is right. Chris and I only see each other on weekends; most of the time. There have been a few weekends where we didn't see each other at all because I was too busy studying or he was doing a show. Next week, I'll be studying for finals, so I won't see him until I go home for the winter holidays the following week.

I have no willpower.

I open the door and yank him inside. I throw my purse onto Senia's bed and throw my arms around him. He laughs when I try to kiss him. Then he starts pushing me away.

"What are you doing?" I whine.

"Hold on, babe. I had something a bit slower planned for us tonight."

He brings his hand forward from behind his back and I smile. He's holding a jar of honey and I can only imagine what he has planned for us.

"I'm gonna turn around and close my eyes. You're going to get naked and hide a dab of this somewhere on your body. Then we're going to turn off the lights and I'm going to try to find it with my mouth."

He hands me the jar and smiles as he turns around. I set the jar on my bed and quickly undress. The obvious place to hide a dab of honey is between my legs, but I think I'll make him work for it.

Once I'm done, I place the jar of honey on the night-stand, still open in case we need more later. Then I lie down on my bed.

"I'm ready."

He turns around and ogles me for a bit, before he reaches under the lampshade and turns off the light. The room isn't completely dark, so I have a nice view as Chris undresses next to the bed. Then he reaches down and traces his finger from my ankle to my center, but he doesn't shove his fingers inside me or caress my clit the way he normally does. He just pulls his hand away, leaving me aching for more.

He sits on the foot of the bed and grabs my ankle.

Bringing my ankle to his mouth, I hold my breath as he licks underneath the arch of my foot. I feel it right in between my legs, as if his mouth is on my aching nub instead.

Then he traces his tongue up to my ankle and lifts my leg straight up in the air. He kisses his way down the back of my leg and I try to remember to breathe. When he reaches the place where the back of my thigh melts into my cheek, he moves to the side and nuzzles his nose against my slit. As if he doesn't want to place his mouth there, to save that spot for later.

He tastes his way up and down my other leg, then he flips me over onto my stomach. He lies on top of me, his erection prodding my backside as he brushes my hair over my shoulder and tastes the back of my neck. He's going to find the honey soon.

He kisses every inch of my neck and shoulders, his hand reaching under me to massage my breast as his erection grinds softly between the outer region of my cheeks. Then he moves down, laying a trail of kisses down my spine until he reaches my lower back. His mouth lingers just above my ass, where I left the dab of honey.

He licks me clean, then he turns me onto my side as he positions himself behind me. His hand reaches forward and quickly finds my clit as he whispers in my ear. "Good job, babe."

I whimper as he continues to massage my pleasure spot.

Then he grabs my thigh and spreads my legs so he can enter from behind.

"How about we skip the spooning and get straight to forking?"

I gasp and laugh at the same time as the tip of his erection hits my cervix. His fingers strum my clit as his other hand slides up and pinches my nipple. He buries his face in my neck and bites me softly.

"You're so fucking hot," he groans.

"Oh, Chris," I cry, as my body begins to tremble. "Don't stop."

He sucks on my earlobe and his breath in my ear sends shiver down my neck. "I love you."

As soon as he murmurs this into my ear, I realize he's not using a condom. I squeeze my eyes shut and and grab his hand to push it back down between my legs. It's too late now.

"I love you," I breathe.

He pulls his hand out from between my legs. "Patience, babe. I'm gonna finish you with my mouth."

We roll over so I'm on all fours and he pounds me from behind. And I try not to worry when he finishes inside me. I just finished my period three days ago. It will be fine.

After he lets go, he immediately flips me onto my back and, through the blue darkness, I can see the grin on his face as he dives between my legs.

"Oh, God."

He parts my flesh with his fingers and licks my clit, softly at first.

He chuckles when he tastes the honey. "I knew you couldn't resist."

"Can you blame me?"

He doesn't answer. He continues to lick away every last bit of honey on my clit — and I put quite a bit — until I scream his name. As usual, he plants a goodbye kiss on the inside of my thigh before he comes up. He lies on top of me and I'm not at all surprised when he enters me again.

I wrap my legs around his hips and squeeze, coaxing him farther inside. He kisses me and I can still taste a hint of honey on his lips. His tongue dances around mine and I feel as if I could do this all night. I'm not at all tired.

His lips move down to the my jaw and then my neck. Then he pushes himself up on his hands so he can look down at me. I run my fingernails up and down his muscular arms as he moves inside me, slowly this time.

"That was fun. We should do that honey thing more often."

He smiles and kisses my forehead. "I could do that with you all day long. I never get tired of licking your skin."

He slides his hand behind my knee and lifts my leg. I whimper as he drives deeper into me, hitting my core. But this position always drives him crazy. And soon he lets go inside me. Again.

After a few more rounds, I dress in my pajamas and he gets dressed in his hoodie and jeans. I hide the honey under my bed, for next time when I get to search for the honey on Chris. Then I walk him to the door.

"I'll be back in the afternoon so we can go to brunch," he says, planting a kiss on my temple.

"Are you sure you don't want to stay the night?"

He laughs. "I wish. I'd go through that whole jar with you tonight, if I could."

Chris has to ride his motorcycle to Durham tonight to pick up a microphone from some guy I've never heard of. Then he has an eight a.m. meeting with Xander, his manager. Not sure why Xander insists on meeting with him on a Sunday morning. But that's Chris's life. It's becoming less and less familiar to me, just like mine is becoming less familiar to him.

FOREVER TROUBLED

CHRIS

MAY, 2012

Claire and Senia are all dressed up and ready to party when I arrive at the dorm. Claire has her hair pulled up into a ponytail. My favorite hairstyle on her. It gives me easy access to her neck.

It seems fitting that she would be dressed up and looking so enticing on a night where I'm more confused about us than I've ever been.

I find myself wanting to touch her. And I try not to think that this is my subconscious fears acting through me. The fear of losing Claire has never been this strong. But it's funny how fear works. It keeps you from doing the one thing that may ease your fear. I can't bring myself to talk to her about this.

She stands next to her desk, digging through the drawer for her lip balm. I sneak up behind her and grab the sides of her waist and she laughs as I press my hips against her.

"Stop it," she protests, pushing my hand off her waist.

"Hey, don't mind me," Senia says from somewhere behind me. "Just give me a sec so I can make some popcorn."

I take a painful step back, away from Claire. I want to tell her that we should stay in and talk, but I need to give myself some time to think. Besides, she's been looking forward to this party for a while.

"Hey, this show isn't free," I say to Senia as a knock comes at the door.

Senia's sitting on her bed, fastening the strap on her heels. "Can you get that, Chris?"

I open the door and greet six-foot-four Kevin Brown with a nod. "What's up, man?"

Kevin enters and we each lean against a desk on opposite sides of the room while we wait for Claire and Senia to finish getting ready. Senia has been through at least four boyfriends since Christmas. Kevin is her latest victim, though Claire would kill me if I said that aloud. Senia has set her drunk self loose on the male population of the University of North Carolina, Chapel Hill, and she's quickly conquering them one by one. But I must admit that it makes for good weekend entertainment.

We walk to Lambda Chi Alpha house on Pickard and Franklin, and we're not surprised to find there's no parking on Pickard or in the parking lot behind the house. The place is crawling with drunk college guys and a few girls here and there. This isn't my crowd. Neither Tristan, Jake, nor I went to college after high school. I try not to let it intimidate me, but it's hard. Especially on a night like this when I've got so much on my mind.

"What's wrong? You're so quiet tonight," Claire says as we climb the porch steps to the front door of the blue two-story house.

"Got some stuff on my mind. Just band stuff. No big deal."

She looks a little worried, but she lets it go and we head inside. Claire knows that the band has been having trouble lately ever since Xander had the bright idea of dropping the band name. Now he books all our shows under Chris Knight instead of Blue Knights. Tristan missed his first show last week and Jake and I had to play without a bassist. He's testing his worth.

But that's the least of my problems right now.

Senia and I have the same idea and we head straight for

the booze. Kevin runs into one of his basketball teammates and they talk basketball while Claire tries to keep Senia and me from getting too shitfaced. But she's doing a poor job.

We down our fifth shot of cherry whiskey — Senia's new favorite drink — and she stares at me for a moment. I'm afraid she's going to puke in my face, so I take a step back and get Kevin's attention. He looks at me questioningly and I nod at Senia. He shakes his head and puts his hand on the small of her back to lead her out of the kitchen.

"Wait! There's still a little left in the bottle."

"There ain't nothing left in that bottle, girl. You're seeing things." She looks over her shoulder, a deep longing in her eyes as she looks at the bottles on the counter. "Come on, baby. You can sit on my lap and take it easy for a little while."

"Ooh. On your lap?"

Their voices fade away the farther they get, until we can't hear or see them anymore. Claire turns to me and she looks pissed. She's probably angry because she knows I have a higher tolerance for alcohol. I should have stopped Senia from trying to keep up with me.

"Why are you drinking so much?"

My face is getting numb and I'm feeling very loose, but I manage to pull out another lie. "I'm just trying to keep up with Senia. I'll stop drinking if you want me to."

She looks disappointed in this response. "I have to go check on her."

I grab her hand before she can leave, then I pull her close to me and whisper in her ear. "I'm sorry."

She turns to me looking utterly confused by my behavior and I feel awful.

"I have to piss. I'll meet you in there." I let her go and she sets off for the other room where Senia and Kevin went.

I head for the hallway and squeeze my way past a group of bodies in the corridor. Then I find the line for the restroom. I ignore the girls who smile at me as they pass. When I come out of the restroom twenty-five minutes later, I'm in no mood to see Joanie Tipton waiting for me.

She stands with her arms crossed over chest and her head tilted, as if she's disappointed that I haven't attempted to say hi to her sooner. Her chubby cheeks don't match her rail-thin body and her pinched eyes just creep me the fuck out.

"Hey, Joanie," I say, nodding as I attempt to get past her.

She steps to the side to block me. "That's it? I haven't seen you in almost a year! How have you been?"

I get a strange urge to tell her I'm not doing well, but I know that's the alcohol. "I'm fine. I gotta go. Claire's waiting for me."

I try to step to the other side, but she mirrors me. "You and Claire are still together? Wow ... I didn't expect that to last."

"What?"

"Oh, I just mean that you probably have girls coming at you from all sides. It must be so hard to stay faithful."

I glare at her for a moment before I realize she's right. "Claire and I are fine."

"Chris?"

I whip my head to the left at the sound of Claire's voice. Claire looks pissed as hell. She doesn't know I had to wait in a long line for the restroom.

"Babe," I call to her, pushing my way past Joanie. "There was a long ass line for the restroom."

She looks at Joanie then back at me. "You didn't look like you were in a hurry." I open my mouth to respond and she cuts me off. "Senia just pissed in Kevin's lap. They broke up and now she's crying on the fucking sofa. We have to leave, but I need you to help me carry her home. Now."

We run into someone else who's leaving at the same time and they agree to give us a ride back to Spencer Hall. Claire and I get Senia into her bed just after midnight. Then we sit on Claire's bed in silence.

"What's wrong with you tonight?" she whispers. "Is the band breaking up?"

I shake my head, then I grab her hand and hold it against my lips. "I don't know."

She coils her arms around my neck and we hold each other for a while. Then we slip beneath the covers to go to sleep. But even with all the alcohol in my body, rest doesn't come easy. I have a feeling nothing is going to come easy after tonight.

FOREVER BLINDSIDED

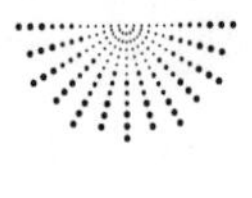

CLAIRE

JUNE 7, 2012

This is the third year Chris and I have spent the anniversary of my mother's death stargazing, and the second year we've done it while camping in Poplar Point. Just like last year, Chris and I made the thirty-minute ride there on his bike.

So what's changed since last year? Chris has a nicer bike now. A blue racing bike that screams sex. I'm no longer a virgin, which means we'll be able to explore each other in addition to exploring the campsite. And, for the first time in about ten months, Chris and I can spend time together without the pressure of homework and music gigs hanging over our heads.

Chris hasn't played a gig in over a month. He's been recording a demo at a local studio up until last week. My freshman year at UNC ended just over a week ago, so I haven't been able to go to the studio with him. Normally, this wouldn't bother me. But I've been getting a weird vibe from Chris whenever he talks about this demo and his trips to the studio. I don't think Chris would lie to me, but I don't know what else to think.

All that matters today is that he's here with me. We're back in a familiar place, physically and mentally. And I have a strong feeling that, by the end of this trip, we'll be back to the way we were emotionally.

We get to the campsite around seven p.m. and Chris quickly sets up our tent, then we skip stones on the lake for a bit while we talk. Chris has tried teaching me to skip stones plenty of times, but I can't seem to get the angle or the right amount of spin on it. I think my record is three skips, while Chris's record is probably a thousand. His rocks dance across the surface of the water as if his touch has embedded them with music.

"I'm going to visit Senia next week. She's picking me up since she's just a couple of miles away."

He smiles as he tosses another stone that skips four times

before it sinks into the water. "Why don't you just drive there?"

"I can't drive your mom's car. I don't have a license."

"So get a license and drive your own car."

I laugh as I toss another stone that immediately sinks below the surface. "Great idea! I'll go get a driver's license next week. Then I'll hop in my imaginary car and go to Senia's."

He turns to me with a sly smile curling his lips. Something about the way the setting sun makes the flecks in his brown eyes turn bright gold takes my breath away.

"I wanted to save this surprise for when we get home, but I might as well tell you now. I got you a car."

"You what?"

"I got you a car. Nothing fancy or new, but it will get you to and from home and school on the weekends next year."

"Why do I need a car for that? I already have Chauffeur Chris."

He chuckles, but it's brief. His face gets very serious all the sudden and I get a pain in my stomach.

"Chris? Why do I need a car?"

He forces his face into a smile, then he grabs my waist and pulls me against him. "I considered getting myself a car so I could go back and forth from the dorm during the rain and snow without freezing my ass off. But then I thought I'd just buy the car for you and I'll keep using my bike."

He buries his face in my neck and I get lost in the sensation of his lips on my skin. I don't question his response.

Chris builds a fire and we eat some roasted hot dogs for a late-night dinner. Then we unzip one of the sleeping bags and lie down in the middle of the campsite to watch the stars. Though Chris says all the right things and he holds me when I get a little emotional about my mom, something feels different. I can't seem to get rid of this knot of pain in the pit of my stomach. This feeling that our opportunity to be Chris and Claire, the way we were before I went to UNC, has passed.

I watch in silence as he checks the inside of the tent for unwanted critters, then he lays down a sleeping bag and spreads out a blanket on top of it. We crawl inside and I lie back as he zips the flap closed. He lies next to me and grabs my hand in the blue darkness.

Before I met Chris, I felt as if I'd been glued to the earth. Heavy as lead and going nowhere no matter how hard I tried to move. Then I met him and I was convinced gravity didn't exist. I felt lighter, as if I could float away like a helium balloon, content to be lost and free. Now the heaviness is returning. Reality is a gravitation pull, yanking us back down to earth when least expect it.

"Do you think the world will ever stop spinning, just so we can catch up?"

His words sound more like a desperate plea than a fleeting question.

I turn onto my side and drape my arm over his bare chest. "Maybe it's not up to the world. Maybe it's up to us to make it stop."

He grabs my hand and brings it to his mouth, laying a kiss on the tips of my fingers. "Let's give it a shot."

He turns onto his side so he's facing me, then he grabs my hip and gently pushes me onto my back. His hand reaches up, his fingers brushing lightly over my jaw, tracing a line over my top lip, down my chin and neck, between my breasts. I suck in a sharp breath as his hand whispers over my belly and lands on the button of my jean shorts.

My skin sizzles with goose bumps as he undoes my button and slides the zipper down, never taking his eyes off mine. I hastily push my shorts and panties down and his gaze is still locked on my face as his hand glides smoothly over my mound. His finger slides inside of me, collecting my wetness like a trophy and bringing it back to my clit as an offering.

He moves his finger in torturously slow circles around my clit as he leans in to whisper in my ear. "Has the Earth stopped spinning yet?"

I arch my back and close my eyes as the world fades to black. "Yes," I reply, my voice shaky.

He kisses my neck and I don't even mind that he's sucking a bit harder than usual. I don't care if he leaves his mark. It's just him and me and the shimmering stars out here tonight. The black sky can swallow us whole and I'd be perfectly happy just to be lost and free with Chris in this moment.

He settles himself between my legs and I feel his velvety smooth erection pressing against my inner thigh. But he doesn't slide into me. He wouldn't be Chris if he didn't take care of me first.

His chest slides over mine as he goes down, positioning himself between my legs. I gasp when his mouth is on me. The soft pads of his lips close around my clit as his warm tongue massages it. I fight the urge to squirm away. My body quivers with lust, my hips bucking until I my limbs are flooded with warm ecstasy and I let go.

He lays a soft kiss on my clit before he moves up to kiss me on the mouth. I'm dizzy with greed as I reach down and curl my fingers around his erection, guiding it inside me. Tightening my legs around his hips, he lets out a sexy groan as he plunges into me.

"You *are* my world," he says, looking me in the eye. "As long as we're together, the world spins for us and no one else. Remember that, okay?"

I nod as I grab his face and pull him toward me to crush my lips to his. His tongue tastes like me and I moan as he thrusts harder, stretching me to accommodate his girth. I tighten my arms around his neck and bury my face in the woodsy scent of his neck, silently wishing we could stay here, in our world, forever.

The next morning, we go for a quick swim in the lake. But, by the time we get back to the campsite, my backpack with all our clothes is gone. Luckily, Chris brought his wallet with us to the lake, but now we don't have any clothes to change into for the ride home.

Chris knows how much I hate getting on the bike without jeans. If he takes a turn too fast, and I'm wearing shorts or a skirt, sometimes I'll burn my leg on the muffler. Nothing serious, but enough for me to be leery of climbing on his bike in a red bikini.

He smiles as he nods over his shoulder and I climb on behind him. "I'll go extra slow and I'll be extra careful," he assures me.

Something about his words, and the feeling of my half-naked breasts pressed against his wet skin....

I reach forward and slide my hand into the front of his shorts. He laughs, but he instantly hardens in my hand. I kiss his back as I close my fist around his erection and slide it back and forth. He's still wet from the lake, making it a little hard for my hand to glide smoothly over his skin. So I move my hand to the head and massage the sensitive place just beneath the tip.

"Jesus Christ," he breathes. "Get off the bike."

I slide off and land with a crunch on the dirt floor.

Immediately, he reaches over and I laugh as he lifts me up onto the seat so I'm facing him. He takes my face in his hands and kisses me hard while I reach between us and push the front of his shorts down to release his erection. Then he slides his hand between my legs, pushes my bikini to the side, and slides into me.

"Oh, God," I cry.

He leans forward and grabs the handlebars of his bike and keeps his feet firmly planted on the ground as he drives into me. I wrap my legs around him and rock my hips in unison with his.

"How do you do this to me?" he growls against my skin as he kisses my neck. "You drive me insane."

I lean my head back and he sucks on the hollow of my throat. I dig my nails into his damp skin as he dives farther into the depths of me. He slides his hand between us and his touch is urgent, a bit rough, as he massages me, but it feels just right. And I come shortly after him.

He holds me tightly in his arms so I don't collapse over the side of the bike. Kissing my shoulders and neck as he softens and slowly slides out of me. He kisses the corner of my lips, then he begins kissing me again; tenderly this time.

I chuckle as I push his shoulders back. "I think once is enough. We should head home."

He looks disappointed. "I …." He lets out a long sigh. "Claire, I got offered a deal."

For a moment, I'm confused, until I realize he's referring to a record deal. Goosebumps sprout all over my body as I'm filled with euphoria.

"That's so amazing! Oh, my God. I'm so happy for you!"

I throw my arms around his neck and squeeze him tight. But he doesn't return my embrace with as much enthusiasm.

"Aren't you excited?"

"Yeah. It's great."

I release him so I can see his face, but he doesn't look at all excited. "Chris, what's wrong?"

He looks me in the eye for a moment, then he drops his gaze and hangs his head. "They want me to go to L.A. for a few months to record the album."

Though the mention of a few months apart sends a shock of pain through my insides, I still don't understand why he looks so upset.

"It's just a few months," I say, lifting his chin so I can see his face. "It will hurt, but we'll get through it. Maybe I can even go with you. It's the summer!"

He flashes me the weakest, most phony smile I've ever seen. And that's when I know something is very wrong.

"It's not just a few months. I'd be leaving on tour pretty soon after that … for eight months."

My limbs get weak and my hands fall from his neck, landing between us. He grabs both my hands and we stay like this for a while, not speaking or looking at each other.

I don't know what he's thinking, but I'm thinking about Chris on tour, by himself, with thousands of girls screaming his name, throwing their bras onto the stage, offering themselves to him. While I'm bored out of my mind in a lecture hall or toiling away on a term paper in the dorm. And that's when I know.

This is the end of us.

FOREVER BROKEN

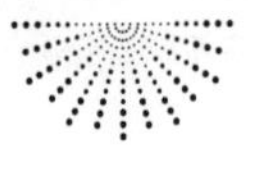

CLAIRE

JULY 14, 2012

Somewhere around eight-thirty, I gather the courage to wake Chris. We've been lying in his bed all night, his arms wrapped around my waist and his head resting on my chest. He dozed off around five a.m., but I've been up all night.

He lifts his head from my chest and squints at me through the hazy morning light. Reaching up, he brushes my hair away from my face then tucks it behind my ear.

"Good morning, babe."

I close my eyes and try to burn the sound of him saying good morning into my memory. When I open my eyes, his eyes are closed. Then he lays his head on my chest again and lets out a soft sigh.

"I don't want to get up."

"You have to," I whisper, running my fingers through his dark hair. "Your mom wants to say goodbye to you."

My voice comes out strangled on the last few words, and Chris notices. He lifts his chin off my chest to look at me, shaking his head when he sees me trying to blink back the tears. He sits up suddenly and leaves the room. He's been doing that a lot lately.

I wipe my face clean and pull my messy bed hair into a ponytail. Then I head out of Chris's room. I wait in the corridor for a moment until he comes out of the restroom. He's wearing nothing but a pair of ragged pajama pants and his hair is sticking out in all directions, but he's still the most beautiful thing I've ever seen.

He presses his lips to my cheekbone then whispers in my ear. "You've broken me."

I turn on my heel and disappear into my room, closing the door quietly behind me so Jackie doesn't know I'm upset. Then I lie in bed and cry for the millionth time in the last six days, since Chris and I — mostly I — decided we should break up. I don't think I could have imagined a worse way to spend this summer.

When I head downstairs twenty minutes later, I see Jackie has made Chris's favorite breakfast: Denver omelet, bacon, and hash browns. Chris looks up from his plate when I enter the kitchen.

"You'd think I was on death row," he remarks as he stabs his fork into a piece of omelet, but he doesn't bring it to his mouth.

Jackie has her back to us as she washes dishes at the sink. I go to her and tap her shoulder. "I'll do those." She shakes her head, but she doesn't speak. "Jackie, are you okay?"

That's when she sniffs loudly and I know she's crying. I wrap my arms around her waist and lay my cheek against her shoulder blade. Her shoulders slump as she stops pretending to be strong.

Finally, she turns around and kisses my forehead. "I have to get going. I know you two want to be alone today."

I nod and try not to cry as I think of the implications behind her words. Jackie's leaving to spend the day at Carolina Beach. She's staying the night at an inn on the coast, then returning tomorrow afternoon. Chris will be gone by then. She's leaving so Chris and I can spend our last day together alone. At home.

Jackie and Chris say their goodbyes outside. When he comes back inside, the sober look on his face is something I'll never get used to. I'm used to seeing Chris with that charming crooked smile. The mischief in his eyes. This dark, dull look is not the Chris I'm used to. Maybe I *have* broken him.

We shower separately and he lies on my bed, staring up at the ceiling, while I brush and blow-dry my hair. When I'm done, we take Mr. Miyagi for a long walk around the neighborhood. I have to stop myself from wondering if this is the kind of thing we'd still be doing when we're in our seventies.

We spend the first five or six hours of our last day together in silence. There's really nothing more to say. We've spent the last month talking, screaming, crying, cursing. There's only one thing left to say, and I'm not sure either of us has the courage to say it.

I sit on the sofa for a while, watching Chris as he tries to play with the dog on the rug. But Mr. Miyagi is either too tired from the long walk or he can sense that Chris is trying to say goodbye. He's not interested. This is too much for Chris.

He stares at the dog for a while, lost in thought. "Why are you making this so hard?"

I don't know if he's talking to me or the dog, so I don't respond.

"Say something, Claire. Anything. Just fucking say something."

I cover my face with my hands and gulp large breaths, trying not to completely fall apart. The sofa cushion tilts as he sits next to me and gravity pulls me into his arms. He holds me so tight it hurts. But it's not enough to drown out the pain in my heart.

I don't know how long we sit like this, but sometime just before sundown we head upstairs to my room. This is it.

"You know we're both going to regret this," he says as he cradles my face in his hands.

"I know, but I don't care."

He kisses me and my entire body relaxes as I lie back on my bed. This is what Chris and I are meant for and I need it just one more time before it's over. I need to feel him moving inside me. I need to feel the weight of him on top of me. I need to feel safe with him one last time.

He lays his palms flat on either side of my head then runs his tongue over my top lip. A chill passes through me and pulses between my legs.

He pulls his head back and looks me in the eye. "I love you, Claire. I'll never stop loving you."

I grab the back of his neck and pull him to me. I wrap my legs around his waist and he grinds against me. There are too many layers of clothing between us. I reach for the button on his jeans and he moves my hand away as he kisses my neck.

"Slow down. We have all night."

His hand slides under my shirt as he gently sucks on my earlobe. I lift my back so he can undo my bra. I hastily peel off my tank top and bra then toss them aside. His fingers move lightly over my stomach until he reaches my breast. I draw in a sharp breath as his mouth covers my nipple. He licks me slowly and torturously, moving from one breast to the other as his hands unbutton my shorts. I lift my hips so he can pull them off, but he leaves my panties on. He takes his shirt and jeans off and tosses them onto the floor before he settles himself between my thighs again.

I can feel him stiff between my legs as his bare chest slides over my breasts. He kisses me and I gasp as his tongue parts my lips and thrusts inside my mouth. I clutch handfuls of his hair to keep his head still. I don't want him to move. I don't want to ever stop kissing him.

He grinds himself against me and my panties are soaked with my need for him. "Please, Chris," I whisper against his lips.

He kisses my neck as his lips travel down to the hollow of my throat. His tongue traces a line straight down my center until his face is between my thighs. He pulls my panties off and pauses for a moment. I look down to see what he's doing and he's staring at me.

"I'm going to miss this," he says, before he kisses me so lightly I can barely feel it.

His fingers part my flesh and he kisses me tenderly, teasing me with feather soft licks. The pleasure builds inside me and I grip the blanket underneath me to keep from writhing.

"Oh, Chris," I moan.

His tongue flicks and torments me into a frenzy and soon I find my release as my body convulses with ecstasy. He lays a soft trail of kisses over my belly and kisses each of my breasts before his mouth is on mine again. He kisses me tenderly as the tears slide down my temples and into my hair.

He pulls his head back and looks down. His boxer briefs are gone and we both watch as he enters me slowly, my mouth opening wide in a silent gasp. I wrap my legs around his waist, beckoning him farther inside.

He takes his time, sinking in and out of me with the ease of a boat bobbing on a calm sea. That's what I am right now. I am a calm sea because the storm hasn't arrived yet. I know everything will be different when Chris leaves, but right now I want to enjoy this small sliver of peace.

He kisses the tears as they slide down my temples. I tighten my arms around his shoulders and crush my lips against his as we both let go … forever?

FOREVER LOST

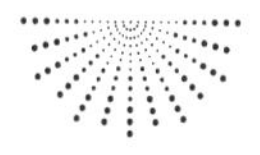

CHRIS

"Are you calling me from a pay phone?"

Claire's voice sounds like a beautiful symphony on the other end of this staticky pay phone.

"I lost my phone at the airport, but I had to call you as soon as I got here." I look around my new L.A. neighborhood. A hot, simmering concrete jungle; lifeless and loveless. "I miss you so fucking much."

"You've been gone ten hours."

"Worst ten hours of my life."

She's silent for a while, then she lets out a soft, forced chuckle. "Hey, want to hear a funny story? Your mom came home this morning with a sunburn. A *bad* sunburn. So I went to the drugstore to get her some aloe vera and the clerk —"

"Claire, I don't think I can do this."

"Do what?"

"Be without you."

Silence again. I'm getting so fucking tired of silence.

"I don't think we should be talking about this," she says, her voice hardly louder than a whisper. "I think you need to give yourself some time to adjust first. Then we can talk about it. You can't throw away all those years of hard work."

It's hard to argue with Claire when she's right. But I still fucking hate that she's right. I want to throw it all away.

"I love you."

"I should go. I have to take the dog for a walk."

"Claire?"

"Yes?"

"Are you still wearing your ring?"

She lets out a soft sigh. "I can't do this, Chris. It hurts too much. Goodbye."

FOREVER TORN

CLAIRE

AUGUST 20, 2012

My phone vibrates on the nightstand and I know it's going to be him. I haven't heard from Chris since the semester began last week. He's been spending fourteen hours a day in the studio. Or so he says.

I slide the phone off the nightstand and stare at Chris's name flashing on the screen. Then I take a deep breath and touch the green button.

"Chris."

"Were you asleep?"

"No, I'm just studying." Lie number one.

"Do you have time to talk?"

"Not really. I'm trying to finish a paper." Lie number two.

"You don't have ten minutes to talk? I want to hear about your week."

I pause for a moment, trying to gather the courage to say what needs to be said. Then I realize I will probably never have the courage. So I might as well just say it.

"Chris, you have to stop calling me."

"Why?"

"Because it's too hard."

"But we agreed to stay friends."

"Friends," I repeat this word with a level of disgust that surprises even me.

"You don't want to be friends with me?"

"That's not what I meant." I try to swallow the lump in my throat, but it's useless. "I don't think that's possible for us. Friends tell each other things, Chris. And … I don't want to know what you're doing."

There's a long, heavy silence where I begin to believe he may have hung up. Then, "Claire?"

"Chris, please. I'm sorry. It just hurts too much. And I want you to do what you want. I don't want to worry about who you're fucking or — "

" — I'm not going to — "

" — Chris, stop."

"I'm coming home."

"Stop! Stop calling me ... *Please!*"

"Claire."

"Stop saying my name. I have to go."

I end the call and throw the phone at the wall so he can't call me back. Then I pull the covers over my head and allow myself to cry. I tell myself that this will be my last day to let myself remember Chris. My last day to revel in the memories and soak my pillow with the tears. This will be the last day.

Tomorrow, we will no longer be Chris and Claire, past, present, or future. Tomorrow, the process of forgetting begins. I don't know how I'll forget the most amazing years of my life. But there's no other way.

I can't let Chris throw away everything he's worked so hard to achieve. Not for me ... or anyone.

FOREVER SHATTERED

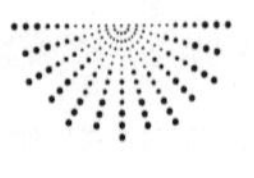

CHRIS

I stare at the phone in my hand, trying to figure out what the fuck just happened. I mean, I knew this was coming. I could hear it in her voice. She's not the same. Neither am I. The distance has killed who we were.

I set the phone down on the kitchen counter in my shitty L.A. apartment. Then I back away from it, as if it's a ticking time bomb. I bump against the oven behind me and that's when I feel it. In my back pocket.

I slide my hand into my pocket and retrieve the glass heart Claire gave me last year. I've carried it with me every day since the day she handed it to me in Moore Square. I read the words engraved on the surface: *ever thine, ever mine, ever ours.*

She wants nothing more to do with me. She probably stopped wearing my ring the day I left.

Fine. If that's the way she wants it.

I hurl the heart across the room and it hits the wall and shatters on the floor in front of the refrigerator.

I came to L.A. because I wanted to follow through on everything I've been working toward since I picked up my first guitar twelve years ago. I never would have quit school and worked my ass off the past three years if I thought this would never happen. But ... I would have thrown it all away for her. For us.

Now I see that she won't let me. Maybe this is easier for her than it is for me. Maybe I was just weighing her down. Taking up her time when she could have been studying or partying. Maybe she's been wanting to breakup for a while.

Staring at the shattered heart, I get a sick thought. Would Claire and I still be together if I had given her an engagement ring instead of a promise ring?

I shake my head at this craziness.

Claire promised to love me forever. I knew forever was too good to be true.

FOREVER ACHING

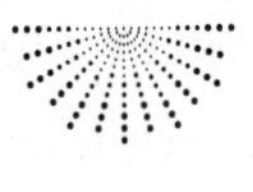

CLAIRE

DECEMBER, 2012

Senia's three-year-old sister, Sophie, has become very good at working the TV remote. Watching her flipping through the channels, her chubby finger pressed on the "plus" button, all I can do is smile. She'll find some cartoon show eventually. Or she'll get tired of holding down the button and give me the remote so I can find the cartoons.

A few seconds later, my prediction comes true. In the worst way possible. She gets tired of pressing the button and she drops the remote into my lap.

"Cartoons," Sophie pleads.

But I can't move. My eyes are glued to the images on the screen. A celebrity gossip show.

"Rocker Chris Knight has been spotted around town with Nicole Priestly, star of this season's blockbuster, *Alive*. Rumors are flying that they were spotted making out in a booth at Triple X, a swanky new restaurant-slash-*strip club* in West Hollywood where all the young celebrities are hanging out these days. Knight's publicist denies the two are anything more than friends. Hmmm... I don't remember the last time I tasted the inside of *my* buddy's mouth."

God, I'm such an idiot!

"Cartoons!"

I've spent the last five months basically lying in bed feeling sorry for both of us. Feeling like we've both suffered with the most difficult decision I ever made; a decision I know I'll always regret. And there he is, shoving his tongue into someone else's mouth. Probably shoving other things in other places, as well. I wouldn't call that suffering.

I knew Chris would move on eventually, but seeing it happen right before my eyes is something else. Now, this nameless girl I imagined him screwing has a face. A very famous face. Imagining his hands on her. His lips on her. His ... *Ugh!* It makes me sick.

"Claire! Cartoons!"

I can't watch TV anymore. That's the only way to avoid this torture.

I pick up the remote and change the channel as Senia walks in with two ice cream sundaes; one for me and one for her.

I shake my head. "I'm not hungry."

"Claire, you have to eat. It's the holidays."

"Ice cream!" Sophie screams.

"This isn't for you," Senia says, and Sophie's bottom lips juts out. Senia rolls her eyes and sets the sundae down on the coffee table in front of Sophie. "You can have a few bites."

Sophie digs into her ice cream and I watch in complete wonderment. How could something as simple as ice cream turn a bad day into a good one for a child? What would turn my bad day into a good one?

Don't answer that question, I chide myself.

FOREVER RESTLESS

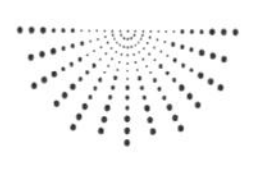

CHRIS

The buzzing noise seeps into my dream and it takes a moment for me to realize it's my phone. I snatch the phone off the bedside table, squinting at the bright screen, and groan when I see the phone number.

"Yeah. I'm awake."

"I should hope so. It's past noon."

I pull the phone away from my ear to look at the time: 12:34 p.m.

"What's up?"

"We need you to come in tonight around seven to re-record some vocals on 'Firefly'." I can tell by the almost bored exasperation in his voice that Gene Hadley is getting tired of re-recording vocals because I was too parched and hungover on the initial recording. "Get some rest and drink plenty of water."

He hangs up and I stare at the screen for a moment as the calls disappears. I swing my legs over the side of the bed and the first thing I see is a black bra on the floor. With great trepidation, I turn my head and peer over my shoulder. I wish I could say I'm surprised to find a thin brunette tangled in my bedsheets. Her left breast is exposed and her pouty lips are slightly parted as she sleeps.

I don't remember what time I got in last night, but I do remember bits and pieces of the party in Tristan's hotel room. Despite the problems with recording, I managed to convince Gene to allow Tristan and Jake to play bass and drums on the tour that kicks off at the end of this month. Tristan and Jake flew out a few days ago and we celebrated having the band back together last night.

It looks like I got a suite in the same hotel for me and … *What's her name again? Laura? Lara? Lorena?* I can't fucking remember.

I rise from the bed slowly and she begins to stir. I freeze for a moment, but she settles down quickly and continues to sleep. I tiptoe out of the bedroom and into the sitting area. Grabbing a bottle of water out of the minibar, I sit down at a glossy mahogany writing desk.

How can it be that it's been five months since I last saw Claire and hers is still the first face I see in my mind when I get the urge to write a song? My memories of Claire are relentless. And no amount of alcohol or sex can erase her.

Picking up the hotel pen and pad of paper, I close my eyes and allow myself to remember. The first thing I see is Claire sitting in the shade of a giant oak tree in Moore Square, smiling as I sing to her. I press the pen to the paper and write the first lines: *We kissed under the trees, and talked about missing things. I wish I could have held you in; held in the heat of your breath; held onto you and I at our best.*

FOREVER OURS

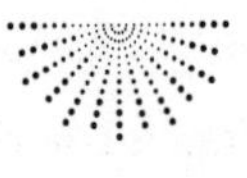

CLAIRE

MAY 27, 2013

It's hard not to think about Chris on his twenty-first birthday. But I'm going to try my hardest not to. I know wherever he is today, he's probably having lots of fun. Drinking lots of booze. Screwing lots of girls. He's living. So that's what I'm going to do today. I'm going to live my life without thinking about Chris.

Senia is moving in next week and we're going to have a great summer. My new apartment in Wrightsville Beach is kind of old and some of the doors and cabinets are swollen with humidity, but it smells like fresh paint. And it's mine.

Dropping out of UNC just may turn out to be the smartest decision I've ever made.

Chris dropped out and look at him now.

Nope! Stop thinking about Chris.

I grab a bottle of water out of the tiny refrigerator that came with the apartment, then I head out the door. I walk through the small parking lot and toward my new workplace: Beachcombers Café. But I don't go inside. I continue down Lumina to the surf shop next door.

A bell jingles as I enter the shop and I'm reminded of the movie *It's A Wonderful Life.* "Every time a bell rings an angel gets his wings." This reminds me of Christmases with my mom and I realize that I didn't just come here to forget Chris. I came here to forget my mother.

Today, a new Claire emerges from the ashes of the fire that burned down every good thing in my life.

The walls of the shop are covered in surf apparel: wet suits, rash guards, board shorts, T-shirts. The floor displays are stacked with everything from surf wax and leashes to energy gum and tourist gifts. The surfboards are all standing up like soldiers behind the counter.

"Can I help you?" asks a young blonde girl with dreadlocks.

"I'm looking for Fallon."

My voice is a bit shaky, but she doesn't seem to notice or

care. Her face lights up when she smiles. She slides off her stool and rounds the counter.

She holds out her hand for me to shake. "I'm Fallon."

Her voice is kind of husky, but it's comforting. I take her hand and shake it lightly. Her skin is a bit rough, but that makes me trust her. Fallon works until her fingers are calloused. Living with Jackie and Chris, seeing the long hours Jackie worked at the bakery and the endless hours of practice Chris would endure to get a song right, I've come to appreciate a strong work ethic as a very desirable quality.

Must stop thinking about Chris.

"Great!" I reply, letting go of Fallon's hand. "I was just wondering … Well, someone told me that you give … Um, I was told that you're a guru or something. I mean, I don't know what to call it. I just … I want to learn to meditate."

She continues to smile serenely as if I'm the millionth person who's walked in here stammering like an idiot and she knows just how to fix it. "I can help you, but are you sure you're ready?"

"What do you mean?"

She tilts her head as her gaze wanders over my face and to the empty space above my hair. "Do you think you're ready to let go of all this?" She waves her hands around my ears as if she can see all my negative thoughts floating around my head. "All this stuff you're carrying, it's heavy. *Real* heavy."

I can smell smoke on her breath and I'm wondering if maybe I made the wrong decision. She's obviously smoking some good stuff. But maybe that's what I need. Not to smoke some good stuff. But maybe I need someone who's willing to do what I'm not willing to do. Maybe she can teach me how to do what I've been unable to do on my own. Maybe she can teach me to forget.

"I don't know if I'm ready," I reply. "But I know I'm desperate. That counts for something, right?"

She purses her lips, which are a bit too pink for her golden skin. "We'll see. Meet me at the shore tomorrow at six a.m. I always start with a surf lesson to get to know you before we attempt meditation."

I search my mind for my work schedule and realize I work at nine a.m. tomorrow. Linda won't mind if I'm late to work. In fact, I'll stop by the café right now and see if I can get someone else to cover my shift. This is too important.

I thank Fallon and leave the shop feeling lighter than I've felt in months. She's right. I was carrying some heavy stuff around. But I already feel it being lifted away.

Now I know what people mean when they say *today is the first day of the rest of my life*. That's exactly how I feel right now. Today, on Chris's twenty-first birthday, my life without Chris finally begins.

Turn the page for a free preview of *Relentless*.

LYRICS

"Forever Ours"

Sun in your hair, ignites my insides,
Glow of your skin, lights me up right,
Touch of your hand, I'm on my knees here,
Begging please, baby just stay near,
Yeah, right here.

'Cause we don't have to go nowhere,
This place is ours, it's everywhere,
Yeah, we can stay,
Stay forever.
Ours.
It'll stay forever ours.

I don't mind, if we stumble and fall,
Just the way we get through it all,
No, I don't care, if you break us down,
'Cause I'll get up, dust you off again,
All over again.

'Cause we don't have to sleep in darkness,
Blast the lights, it's ours, there's no one else,
It's only me and you,
This is forever.
Ours.
It'll stay forever ours.

"Sleepyhead"

Feels so wrong to want this
You look so broken there
A flicker in the mist
As tired as the air

Your head upon the pillow
It's time to bury bones
Outside a whispering willow
The limbs fall like stones

So frightened of the dark
You're my sleepyhead
Hiding with the stars
Put your dreams to bed
My sleepyhead.
You're my sleepyhead.

With eyes full of shadow
And a mouth full of glass
Gasps come so hollow
Your lips taste like ash

Don't waste your hours
Your time don't come cheap
Don't fall apart, baby
Just fall asleep

And I don't know why I can't kill this doubt
But I promise I'll put your pain to rest
If it means I never sleep again.

PREVIEW OF RELENTLESS

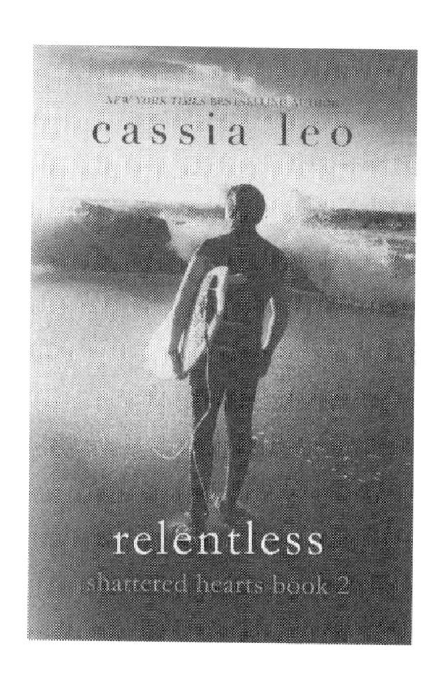

Relentless Addiction

Mom is too tired to play hide-and-seek. Her stomach hurts so she took some medicine to make it feel better. I don't like it when she's sick. Grandma Patty doesn't know about Mom's stomachaches and I haven't seen Grandma in a few weeks, but I'm starting to think I should tell her.

Mom is asleep on the sofa; at least, I think she's asleep. I can't really tell the difference anymore. Sometimes, when I think she's sleeping, I'll try to sneak some cookies out of the cupboard. She usually hears me and yells at me to get out of the kitchen. Sometimes, she sleeps with her eyes half-open so I wave my hands in front of her eyes and make silly faces at her. She never wakes up and I always get bored after a couple of minutes. It's no fun teasing someone unless there's someone else around to laugh, and it's just Mom and me here.

Her skinny arm is stretched out over the edge of the sofa cushion and I stare at the bandage. It's too small to cover that big sore. One of those things she calls an abscess *opened last night while she was making me a grilled-cheese sandwich. Some thick, brown stuff oozed out of her arm. It reminded me of the glaze on maple donuts, but it didn't smell anything like a maple donut. The whole kitchen smelled like stinky feet when she put her arm under the water in the sink. Then she wrapped a billion paper towels around her arm and I had to eat a burnt sandwich.*

She didn't want to go to the doctor. She said that if she goes to the emergency room and shows them her arm the doctors might make her stay in the hospital for a long time. Then I'll have to live with people I don't know, people who might hurt me, until she gets better. My mom loves me a lot. She doesn't want anybody to hurt me the way she was hurt when she was nine.

Mom teaches me a lot. She isn't just my mom; she's my teacher. When she isn't sick, she teaches me math and spelling, but my favorite subject is science. I love learning about the planets the most. I want to be an astronomer when I grow up. Mom said that I can be anything I want to be if I just keep reading and learning. So that's what I do when she's sick. I read.

She's been asleep for a long time today. I've already read two chapters in my science book. Maybe I should try to wake her up. I'm hungry. I can make myself some cereal – I am *seven – but Mom promised she'd make me spaghetti today.*

I slide off the recliner and land on the mashed beige carpet that Mom always says is too dirty for me to sit on. I take two steps until I'm standing just a few inches away from her face. Her skin looks weird, sort of grayish-blue.

"Mom?" I whisper. "I'm hungry."

Something smells like a toilet and I wonder if it's the stinky abscess on her arm. I shake her shoulder a little and her head falls sideways. A glob of thick, white liquid spills from the corner of her mouth.

The memory dissolves as someone calls my name.

"Claire?"

The cash register comes into focus as the rich aroma of espresso replaces the acrid stench in my memory. I've done it again. For the third time this week, I've spaced out while taking someone's order. The last two customers were understanding, but this guy in his *Tap Out* T-shirt and veins bulging out of his smooth bald head looks like he's ready to jump over the counter and either strangle me or get his own coffee.

"Sorry, about that. What was your order?"

"Wake the fuck up, blondie. I asked for an Americano with two Splendas. Jesus fucking Christ. There are people with serious jobs who need to get to work."

I take a deep breath, my fingers trembling, as I punch the order in on the touchscreen. "Will that be all?"

Baldy rolls his eyes at me. "And the scone. Come on, come on. I gotta get the fuck out of here."

"Hey, take it easy. She's just trying to take your order," says a voice. I don't look up, but I can hear it came from the back of the line of customers.

"I already gave her my order three fucking times," Baldy barks over his shoulder. "Mind your own fucking business."

Linda comes up from behind me, placing a comforting

hand on my shoulder as she sets the guy's Americano on the counter next to the bag holding his multigrain scone. She doesn't say anything, but the nasty look she casts in his direction could make an ultimate fighting champion piss his pants. Linda is the best boss in the world and one of the many reasons I still work at *Beachcombers Café*. All the other reasons I still work at one of the tiniest cafés in Wrightsville Beach have to do mostly with my desire to disappear after dropping out of UNC Chapel Hill ten months ago. But that's a whole other story.

Baldy peels the lid off his coffee, rolling his eyes as he peers into the cup. "I said I wanted room for cream. Are you all fucking retarded?"

Before I could reach for the cup, a guy in a suit steps out of line, grabs the cup off the counter, and dumps the entire contents into Baldy's scone bag. A loud collective gasp echoes through the café.

"Now you've got plenty of room for cream," the guy says.

I clap my hand over my mouth to stifle a laugh as Linda scrambles to get some paper towels.

The rage in Baldy's eyes is terrifying. "You motherfucker!" he roars as my white knight grins.

And what a sexy white knight he is. Even in his pressed shirt and slacks, he can't be more than twenty-two. He has an easygoing vibe about him, as if he'd rather be surfing than wearing a suit at seven in the morning. With his sun-kissed brown hair and the devious gleam in his green eyes, he reminds me of Leonardo DiCaprio in one of my favorite movies, *Titanic*.

Baldy charges my Jack Dawson, but Jack swiftly steps aside at the last moment. Baldy trips spectacularly over a waist-high display of mugs and coffee beans. All six people in the café are now standing silent as Baldy spits curses at the cracked mugs and spilled beans underneath him.

I look at my white knight and he's smiling at me, a sneaky half-smile, and I know what he's about to do.

Before Baldy can get to his feet, Jack drops a few hundred-dollar bills on the counter. "For the damages."

He winks at me as he steps on Baldy's back then hurries toward the exit with no coffee, just a huge grin that makes everybody laugh and cheer. He gives us a quick bow, showing his appreciation to the crowd, and slips through the door as Baldy lumbers to his feet.

My gaze follows Jack as he slides into his truck, one of the newer models that looks like something conceived in the wet dreams of a roughneck and a *Star Wars* geek. He pulls out of the parking lot and disappears down Lumina Avenue.

I have a strong urge to whisper, "I'll never let go, Jack," but I'm pretty good at keeping my urges to mutter lines from *Titanic* to myself; especially when there's a six-foot-two 'roided-out freak staring me down. Something snaps inside me as I remember what started this whole fiasco.

I step aside so Linda can take over and I skitter away through the swinging door into the stockroom. I unfold a metal chair and sit down next to a small desk where Linda does the scheduling. Pulling my legs up, I sit cross-legged on the chair, place my hands on my knees, and close my eyes. I take a long, deep breath, focusing on nothing but the oxygen as it enters my lungs. I let the breath out slowly. A few more deep breaths and the whole incident in the café never happened.

Some people are addicted to heroin. Others are addicted to coffee. I'm addicted to meditation. No, not medication. Meditation.

Meditation doesn't just relax me; it helps me forget. It's like a friend you can count on to say just the right thing at the right time when that thing you want them to say is nothing. Meditation is the friend who intervenes when you're about to say or do something very stupid. Like three months ago, when meditation saved me from taking my own life after I realized I had become my mother.

Relentless Memories

I haven't been to a party with my best friend Yesenia

Navarro in ten months. The last time was the Halloween bash at Joey Nassau's house where I got stuck talking to Joey's thirty-something cousin who spent three hours attempting to convince me to go back to school. I want to go to tonight's party at Annabelle Mezza's house about as much as I want to eat a spoonful of cinnamon. Tonight's party will be packed with all the people I have been successfully avoiding for ten months.

"I'll be velcroed to your side the whole night," Senia assures me as I gather my purse and a bottle of water from the kitchen counter.

Senia thinks I'm a freak because I never leave the apartment without at least one bottle of water. I've spent enough time avoiding the various other substances my mother abused. She could hardly call an addiction to water and meditating a bad thing. This doesn't stop her from trying. And true to best-friend form, every day when she comes home from work she still brings me a six-pack of my drug of choice. To say that I love living with my best friend would be a huge understatement.

"Whatever," I mutter. "It's just down the street. I'll walk home if things get too uncomfortable."

"Speaking of uncomfortable." Senia cocks an eyebrow as she examines my outfit: faded skinny jeans, a plain white tank top, a green hoodie that's three sizes too big, and a five-year-old pair of black Converse. "Is that what you're wearing?"

Senia could be a supermodel with her perfectly tanned skin, dark tousled hair, and spot-on fashion sense. At five-ten, she towers over my five-foot-six frame in her four-inch heels. She has the perfect button nose and full lips that I've always dreamed of having. My blonde hair is too thin, my nose is too small, and my upper lip is too big. Senia says it gives me a sexy pout, but she only says that to make me feel better. I'm average and I've learned to not only accept it, I embrace it.

"Don't make me say it," I reply as I unscrew the cap on the bottle of water and take a swig.

She holds up her hand to stop me. "Please don't. And, by the way, that has to be the *worst* motto ever adopted by any person ever in the history of all mankind."

I pull my keys out of my purse to lock the front door as we make our way out of the apartment. "You might be exaggerating just a little bit."

Her heels click against the pavement and I inhale a huge breath of briny ocean breeze as we walk to the covered parking spot where Senia keeps her new black Ford Focus. She isn't rolling in cash, but her parents make pretty good money with the real-estate company where their entire family works. She works in one of their satellite offices in Wilmington while the rest of the family works at the main office in Raleigh. Her parents pay her half of the rent on our apartment, her entire UNC tuition, and she gets a new car every two years on her birthday. Nothing fancy, but new.

"I get it," Senia says as she deactivates her car alarm and we slide into our seats. "You don't want to be a shallow, vacuous piece of shit like Joanie Tipton. But that doesn't mean that you have to dress for a party like you're going to work on a fucking construction site."

"Hey, I resent that. I left my tool belt at home this time," I tease her and she rolls her eyes as she turns on the stereo to her favorite EDM station.

An Ellie Goulding dance mix blasts through the speakers and Senia immediately begins bobbing her head as she pulls the car out of the parking space. She maneuvers her car around the moving truck that's half-blocking the exit out of the complex. Cora, our eighty-six-year-old landlord, must have finally found a tenant for the upstairs apartment.

"Claire!" Senia shouts as she pulls onto Lumina. "You need to renew your driver's license!"

"Senia! I live four hundred feet from where I work and I don't have a car. I don't need a driver's license just so I can be your designated driver."

I sold my car when I moved to Wrightsville Beach two and a half months ago to pay for the first and last month's rent on my apartment. Senia moved in three weeks later, once the semester ended. She claimed she did it so we could spend the summer together on the hottest surf beach on the East Coast, but I know it's so she can help me with the rent for a few months. The summer is halfway over now and she'll be moving back in with her parents in a month to go back to UNC. If I don't find another roommate or convince Linda to give me more hours at the café, I may be homeless in six months – for the third time in my life.

As soon as Senia pulls up in front of Annabelle's parents' beach house, I smell the beer and hear the laughter. My chest tightens. I focus my eyes on the water bottle in my hand, forcing myself to think of nothing else as I breathe deeply and slowly. Senia is quiet as she waits for me. She's used to my coping mechanisms.

The edges of my vision blur and everything but the bottle disappears. I think about how water is the essential element for life to flourish. I think of how it soothes and carries us, cleanses and quenches us. I imagine the water washing away every worry, every doubt about tonight and carrying it away to a clear, tranquil sea. I close my eyes and take one final deep breath as my muscles go slack and I'm completely relaxed.

I nod once and reach for the door handle. "Okay. Let's do this."

"I don't know how you do that, but it's kind of creepy and inspiring all at once."

Senia and I stroll up the walkway arm-in-arm past the

lush summer garden toward the blue, two-story clapboard beach house. I spot a group of five guys standing on the porch with red Solo cups and cigarettes clutched in their hands. From his profile, I recognize the short Indian guy leaning against the porch railing. He was in the sophomore Comp Lit class I dropped out of last October. I turn my head slightly as Senia and I climb the steps to the front door, hoping none of them will recognize me.

Senia pulls open the squeaky screen door and I choke on the sweet smell of alcohol and perfume. We step further inside and the first thing I see is a gathering of a dozen or so people huddled around the sofa where a guy with a guitar is playing and singing a Jason Mraz song.

This memory is too strong to fight.

I walk through the tall door into my ninth and final foster home. As luck would have it, the woman I called Grandma Patty eight years ago was actually just our closest neighbor. I had no family to take me in after my mother died. I'm only fifteen, but I'm already more jaded and cynical than my forty-something caseworker. She flat out told me that this would be my last placement. If I screw this one up, I'll be sent to a halfway house until I turn sixteen in four months. The moment I step into the living room, I know I'll be seeing the inside of that halfway house soon.

Three guys sit around a coffee table, two of them on

the sofa and one cross-legged on the floor with a guitar in his lap. The one with the guitar wears a gray beanie and his dark hair falls around his face in jagged wisps. He's humming a tune I recognize as a Beatles song my mom used to play whenever she cleaned the house: "I Want You."

The thud of my backpack hitting the floor gets his attention and he looks straight into my eyes. "Are you Claire?" he asks. His voice is smooth with just a touch of a rasp.

I nod and he immediately sets his guitar down on the floor in front of him. My body tenses as he walks toward me – as my "training" kicks in. The reason I've been in and out of foster homes for the past eight years since my mom OD'd is because of everything she taught me.

From as far back as I can remember, my mother taught me never to trust men or boys. She was so honest and candid with me about the things her uncle did to her from the time she was nine until she was fourteen. She told me all the things to look out for, all the promises these predators would make. The most important thing to remember, she told me, was to never let them think you were a victim because that was when they pounced.

I followed my mom's advice for eight years and I hadn't been so much as hugged the wrong way. I'd kept myself safe, but only by getting myself kicked out of every foster home at the slightest hint that someone might see me as prey. This guy in the beanie doesn't look like a predator, but looks can be deceiving.

He grabs the handle of my backpack and nods toward the stairs. "I'm Chris. I'll take you to your room."

Senia shakes my arm and the living room comes back into focus. "Are you okay?"

I nod quickly and she gives me a tight smile. She knows what just happened, but she's willing to shrug it off because she knows that's exactly what I need tonight. No long talks about getting over the past or seeing a shrink. People have endured far worse than I have. There's devastating famine and wars being waged across the globe. I have nothing to complain about – except the fact that I really don't want to be here tonight.

I spend the entire night hiding my face every time someone I recognize enters the room or explaining how I dropped out because I couldn't pay my student loans. No one here knows the truth. The one smart thing I did last year was drop out before word could spread around campus.

At twenty minutes past midnight, Joanie Tipton finally enters the living room and casts a lazy smile in my direction, and *now* it's time to leave. Joanie is the only person here, besides Senia, who knows why I dropped out. I had to beg Joanie, on my knees, not to tell anybody. It was the second most humiliating moment of my life.

I grab Senia's arm and whisper into her ear, "Don't look now. Mr. Jones just arrived. I have to get out of here."

Mr. Jones is the nickname Senia gave Joanie after she got a chin implant the summer before our sophomore year and we decided she now looks like a transvestite version of Bridget Jones. She even has Renee Zellweger's scrunched eyes. It would be funnier if she didn't hold my secret in her French-manicured hands.

"I'll take you home," she whispers back and I shake my head adamantly.

"No! I'm just going to sleep. You don't need to come home for that. I'll walk."

Her eyebrows furrow and she nods. "Breaking all the rules tonight, huh?" She's referring to the fact that I never walk the streets alone at night. "I know you're sleeping in so I guess I'll see you when I get back on Monday. Love you."

I kiss the top of her head as I rise from the sofa and scoot past her. I glare at Joanie from across the room as I leave, though she isn't looking at me. She's already engaged in a flirtation with a guy who's at least ten years older than us. God, I wish I had a secret on her.

I duck out of the house and pretend to adjust my bangs as I pass a couple making out next to a car in the driveway. The last thing I need is to be recognized as I'm leaving. As soon as I'm out of the couple's line of sight, I pick up my pace. Our apartment is only two and a half blocks away. The only reason Senia drove here is because of her monstrous heels.

I rush out into the crosswalk, eager to get away from the party – and the memories. I don't see the headlights until it's too late.

To purchase *Relentless*, please visit:

cassialeo.com/shatteredhearts

THANK YOU!

Thank you for reading *Forever Ours*!

If you're enjoying this series, sign up for Cassia's newsletter here to find out more about her next book and never miss any exclusive deleted scenes or bonus content.

Or text BOOKLOVE to 41411 to get a short and sweet text notification when her next book is released.

Purchase signed books and merchandise at cassialeo.com. FREE signed bookmark with every order.

Follow Cassia on Facebook and Twitter to stay up to date on all new books and series. Sign up for email updates on Cassia's blog or become part of her street team to get inside information on new releases, exclusive street team giveaways, and more.

Connect with Cassia:

cassialeo.com

ALSO BY CASSIA LEO

CONTEMPORARY ROMANCE

Stand-alones

Break

Her Guardian

Black Box

The Story of Us Series

The Way We Fall (Book #1)

The Way We Break (Book #2)

The Way We Rise (Book #3)

To Portland, With Love (Book #3.5)

Shattered Hearts Series

Forever Ours (Book #1)

Relentless (Book #2)

Pieces of You (Book #3)

Bring Me Home (Book #4)

Abandon (Book #5)

Chasing Abby (Book #6)

Ripped (Book #7)

ROMANTIC SUSPENSE

Shoot for the Heart Series

Dirt (Book 1)

Seed (Book 2)

Bloom (Book 3)

Power Players Series

Luke

Knox

Chase

Unmasked Series

Unmasked: Volume 1

Unmasked: Volume 2

Unmasked: Volume 3

ROMANTIC COMEDY

Anti-Romance

Edible: The Sex Tape (A Short Story)

PARANORMAL ROMANCE

Carrier Spirits Duet

Parallel Spirits (Book #1)

Kindred Spirits (release date to be announced)

For more information, please visit

cassialeo.com/books

ABOUT THE AUTHOR

New York Times bestselling author Cassia Leo loves her coffee, chocolate, and margaritas with salt. When she's not writing, she spends way too much time re-watching *Game of Thrones*. When she's not binge watching, she's usually enjoying the Oregon rain with a cup of coffee and a book.

How to Support Cassia:

Follow Cassia on BookBub at bit.ly/cassiabookbub to stay up to date on all new releases, preorders, and sales.

Sign up to be a VIP reader at cassialeo.com/news. VIP readers get emails with bonus content, exclusive giveaways, excerpts from books before they're released, and special sales and events.

Like Cassia on Facebook at fb.com/authorcassialeo, and follow her on **Twitter at @authorcassialeo** to stay up to date on all new books and series. If you want to know what Cassia eats for breakfast, lunch, and dinner, follow her on **Instagram at @cassialeo**. And don't forget to **join Club Cassia at cassialeo.com/team** to get access to ARCs, exclusive giveaways, teasers, and more!

Post your review of ***The Story of Us: The Complete Series* on Goodreads**!

Send Cassia some love at:

cassialeo.com/contact

contact@cassialeo.com

Made in the USA
Middletown, DE
26 February 2019